"Use any excuse you have to. Just get your dad there," Zoe told Kristy.

"My mom's taking the night off from the restaurant, and I've already got the romantic music picked out.

"Plan B, we fight in school. Both parents will have to meet to take care of that.

"Plan C, is the Girl Scout field trip to the beach next weekend. I've already fixed it with the troop leader so your dad and my mom will have to be in the same car and spend the whole day together chaperoning. And remember, our whole plan will be ruined if my mom finds out what your dad's job is, so we have to keep quiet about that, okay?"

"I don't want to do Plan X, Zoe."

"It's last-ditch, only if nothing else works. And it's not gonna happen anyway."

Zoe was right as usual.

It was time to invent a family however they could.

Dear Reader,

After looking at winter's bleak landscape and feeling her icy cold breezes, I found nothing to be more rewarding than savoring the warm ocean breezes from a poolside lounge chair as I read a soon-to-be favorite book or two! Of course, as I choose my books for this long-anticipated outing, this month's Silhouette Romance offerings will be on the top of my pile.

Cara Colter begins the month with *Chasing Dreams* (#1818), part of her A FATHER'S WISH trilogy. In this poignant title, a beautiful academic moves outside her comfort zone and feels alive for the first time in the arms of a brawny man who would seem her polar opposite. When an unexpected night of passion results in a pregnancy, the hero and heroine learn that duty can bring its own sweet rewards, in *Wishing and Hoping* (#1819), the debut book in beloved series author Susan Meier's THE CUPID CAMPAIGN miniseries. Elizabeth Harbison sets out to discover whether bustling New York City will prove the setting for a modern-day fairy tale when an ordinary woman comes face-to-face with one of the world's most eligible royals, in *If the Slipper Fits* (#1820). Finally, Lissa Manley rounds out the month with *The Parent Trap* (#1821), in which two matchmaking girls set out to invent a family.

Be sure to return next month when Cara Colter concludes her heartwarming trilogy.

Happy reading!

Ann Leslie Tuttle
Associate Senior Editor

Please address questions and book requests to:
Silhouette Reader Service
U.S.: 3010 Walden Ave., P.O. Box 1325, Buffalo, NY 14269
Canadian: P.O. Box 609, Fort Erie, Ont. L2A 5X3

The
PARENT
TRAP
LISSA MANLEY

SILHOUETTE *Romance*®
Published by Silhouette Books
America's Publisher of Contemporary Romance

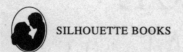 SILHOUETTE BOOKS

ISBN 0-373-19821-3

THE PARENT TRAP

Copyright © 2006 by Melissa A. Manley

Printed in U.S.A.

Books by Lissa Manley

LISSA MANLEY

has been an avid reader of romance since her teens and firmly believes that writing romances with happy endings is her dream job. She lives in the beautiful Pacific Northwest with her college-sweetheart husband of nineteen years, Kevin, two children, Laura and Sean, and two feisty toy poodles named Lexi and Angel, who run the household and get away with it. She has a degree in business from the University of Oregon, having discovered the joys of writing well after her college years. In her spare time, she enjoys reading, crafting, attending her children's sporting events and relaxing at the family vacation home on the Oregon coast.

Lissa loves to hear from her readers. She can be reached at P.O. Box 91336, Portland, OR 97291-0336, or at http://lissamanley.com.

This book is dedicated to my two writing consultants, Lexi and Angel, who were there by my side as I wrote every word. And also to Jade, my consultant-in-training, who will join them on the couch as I write the next book.
Thanks for the company, girls.

Prologue

"Are you sure this is going to work, Zoe?" Kristy Clark asked, chewing on her thumbnail. Kristy desperately wanted to believe her new best friend's plan to invent a family would work, but wondered if she was stupid to try to get her dad to fall in love. He never even went out on any dates or anything.

Zoe Lindstrom rolled her blue eyes as she yanked a frilly white wedding dress onto her Malibu Barbie. "Sure it's going to work. We're inventors, just like my grandpa."

"But do you really think we can make a family?" Kristy shifted on the porch stairs as she tried to pull a plastic comb through her Skipper doll's tangled brown hair so Skipper would look good in her flower-girl outfit. "Isn't it kind of…well, impossible?" To

Kristy, an instant family, complete with built-in sister, seemed like a little too much to hope for. And having a mom…well, that was just a dream, a beautiful fantasy, really.

But, oh, the thought of having a mom she could talk to about girl stuff and go shopping with! Sure, her dad was great. But he was a man. What did he know about the coolest nail polish colors?

Zoe sifted through the shoe box full of Barbie clothes on the porch stairs, pulling out a Barbie-sized wedding veil and tiny white satin shoes. "I don't have a dad, you don't have a mom. Your dad is so funny, and my mom likes to laugh, and they both like to work out and they both own restaurants. They're perfect for each other. How hard can it be?" She plopped the veil on Barbie's head, then shoved the shoes on her feet.

"But what if they don't fall in love?" Kristy wanted a whole family more than anything, but her dad had to love the woman he married, if he ever did manage to find someone he was interested in. That seemed pretty impossible right now. She was only eight, but it wasn't hard to see that he still really missed her mom, even though it'd been seven years since she died and went to heaven.

Zoe flipped her blond hair over her shoulders and gave her an exasperated look. "Would you relax? Everything'll work out fine as long as we follow my grandpa's formula. Make a plan. Go over the plan again. Ex…um…oh, yeah, execute. Execute again if we have to." She smiled and held up her Barbie, who was decked out for a wedding. "As long as we don't blow anything up like my grandpa usually does, everything will be okay."

Kristy wished she could be as sure about all of this as Zoe was. Zoe was so cool, so confident, so much fun. All the things Kristy longed to be.

Maybe going over The Plan would help. "So Plan A comes first, right?" Kristy asked.

Zoe nodded. "Right. Plan A, dinner at my house tomorrow night. Use any excuse you have to, just get your dad there. My mom's taking the night off from the restaurant, and I've already got the romantic music picked out."

"Gotcha." Kristy fiddled with the end of her braid, admiring how well Zoe had planned all of this. "Then Plan B, right?" She wasn't hot on Plan B, but would do it if it helped invent her a family.

"Right again. Plan B, we fight at school. Both parents will have to meet to take care of that."

"Plan C after that."

"Yup. Plan C, Girl Scout field trip to the beach next weekend. I've already fixed it with the troop leader so your dad and my mom will have to be in the same car and spend the whole day together chaperoning. My grandpa told my mom he needs her car that day, so she can't offer to drive herself. And remember, our whole plan will probably be ruined if my mom finds out what your dad's job is and if your dad finds out what my mom's job is, so we have to be quiet about that, okay?"

"Okay." Kristy swallowed hard. "And then...Plan X."

Zoe gazed at her, suddenly looking serious. "Plan X is last-ditch, only executed if nothing else works."

"I don't want to do Plan X," Kristy said, biting her lip. Her dad would ground her for life if she actually went through with it.

Zoe put her hand on Kristy's arm and squeezed. "Don't worry about Plan X. It's not gonna happen." She picked up her Ken doll and adjusted his black tuxedo. "But if it does, it'll be okay. We'll be safe the whole time, Kris. No one will get hurt."

Kristy hoped so. She wanted to invent a family a lot, but Plan X made her kind of nervous.

Too bad. She was determined to be more like Zoe. Confident. Fearless. Sure of herself and their plan.

"This is my mom, and this is your dad," Zoe said, picking up Bride Barbie and Groom Ken. Then she gently pressed them together as if they were kissing, her mouth curling into a huge smile. "We can do this, Kris. If we want to be a family, we have to."

Zoe was right, as usual.

It was time to invent a family however they could.

Chapter One

"Here, Mom, put this on."

Jill Lindstrom put down the lasagna she'd just taken out of the oven, then swung around and met her nine-year-old daughter Zoe's excited gaze. Zoe had a bottle of Jill's favorite perfume held high, her finger on the spray button, ready to blast Jill in the face with the scent.

Jill quickly danced back a step, out of spray range, then raised an eyebrow, dubiously regarding the bottle of perfume. "Geez, Zoe, watch where you point that stuff."

Zoe rolled her eyes. "Just put some on."

"I already put perfume on this morning," Jill said, moving to the fridge to take out the Caesar salad she'd made earlier. "I don't need any more."

"C'mon, Mom—"

Jill held up a hand. "Look, I already wore the jeans and sweater you set out, and I left my hair down as you so forcefully demanded." She put the salad down and went in search of the salad tongs. "I'm drawing the line at excessive amounts of perfume. We want to welcome Kristy and her dad, not knock them out with loads of Ralph Lauren."

Zoe huffed, flicked her blond hair over her shoulder and spun around to leave the kitchen. "Okay, Mom. I'll be waiting in the living room."

Jill watched her go, shaking her head, one side of her mouth quirked. It certainly didn't take a genius to figure out that Zoe was very, very concerned that Jill look—and apparently smell—her best. Similarly, she suspected it was no coincidence that Kristy's father was single, just as Jill was.

Looked as if Zoe and her new best friend were up to a little matchmaking. Was that thanks to the influence of Zoe's grandpa? Zoe absolutely adored her grandpa, and he had made no secret of his desire to see Jill married again.

Jill rolled her eyes. No matter who was involved, any matchmaking was a waste of time. Even though it had been six years since her ex-husband, Doug, had left her for another woman, she still wasn't ready to put her heart, and self-respect, on the line again. She might never be.

Jill returned to the fridge and dug out the salad dressing and Parmesan cheese. As she gathered up the salad plates, she reiterated to herself how important it was that she not get sucked into any sort of relationship. And not just because she wasn't ready to open herself up to again being ditched when someone better came along. Although that was a darn good reason all on its own.

No, she also needed to focus on her restaurant, The Wildflower Grill, and make it a success, an elusive dream she was determined to catch and hold on to.

Jill took the salad fixings to the dining-room table, her mind going over familiar territory, fueling her desire to become a successful, well-respected businesswoman.

She was so tired of being known only as the daughter of "Wacky" Winters, Elm Corners, Oregon's resident inventor. The goofy guy with wild hair and thick, horn-rimmed glasses who ran around wearing a soot-stained apron and bright red hiking boots. Being the only relative of a man who blew up new inventions—and everything else he touched—on a regular basis wasn't easy.

Jill returned to the kitchen, a flash of guilt sizzling through her. She wasn't proud of the way she felt about her dad's status in town, but there it was.

He wasn't a bad man. He'd single-handedly raised Jill since her mother had died when Jill was three—not an easy task—and had always been there when she'd needed him. But there was no getting around the fact that he was the town joke, and she'd always lived in that shadow. Doug leaving her hadn't helped. It was past time to step out into the light, make something of herself and gain the respect she'd never had. Owning a successful restaurant, being a valued member of Elm Corners' business community was just the way to do that.

She bit her lip, well-known worries running through her like a dark tide. She'd slid back in her efforts to step up to the next level of success and finally expand her restaurant as she'd been wanting to do for the past few months.

Last week, the recently vacated space next door to her restaurant had been snapped up by someone before Jill could negotiate a lease. Just her luck that someone else would not only be opening another restaurant a mere two doors down, but also that they had been able to snatch the coveted lease out from under her nose. She had a mind to march right over to The Steak Place and give the new owner a piece of her mind.

Just as she picked up the lasagna to take it to the table, the doorbell rang. Following Zoe's specific instruction that Jill be the one to answer the door—boy, she'd raised a bossy kid—Jill dropped the lasagna off in the dining room, then headed to the front door, meeting an excited-looking Zoe there. Jill calmed the flurry of butterflies that had taken up residence in her tummy. It had been a long time—forever, actually—since a man other than her father had come to dinner.

She was being ridiculous worrying, though. She had no reason to be nervous. This was dinner with her daughter's best friend and her dad, nothing more.

Jill had agreed to the dinner because it was important that she become acquainted with the people her daughter spent time with. Maybe it was overprotective, but besides her dad, Zoe was Jill's only family, the single most important person in her life. She'd protect her no matter what, even if it meant agreeing to invite to dinner a man she'd never met. They'd enjoy a nice meal, and that would be that.

Besides, Kristy's dad—what had Zoe said his name was?—might be a short, middle-aged balding guy with bad breath and a paunch. Suited her just fine.

Putting on a smile, she opened the door to greet Kristy and her dad, vaguely noticing that Zoe had jumped forward to pull Kristy into the house.

Jill momentarily lost the ability to speak when she saw the tall, well-built, attractive man standing next to Kristy, the setting sun at his back.

Not balding. Not short. No paunch in sight. Early thirties, if her guess was right. And while she couldn't possibly tell from this distance, she was pretty sure a guy who looked as good as Kristy's dad did—all brown, wavy hair, dark, seductive eyes and broad shoulders—wouldn't have bad breath.

Okey-dokey. So he was her fantasy man come true in the looks department, and she'd always been a sucker for a handsome guy. Didn't matter.

She couldn't let it.

* * *

A bottle of red wine in one hand, Brandon Clark stared at the tall, breathtakingly pretty blonde in the doorway, waiting for her to speak. She stared back, her blue eyes wide and unblinking in the light of the setting, early-autumn sun.

"You must be Zoe's mom." He extended his free hand, initiating the introductions, since she wasn't saying anything. "I'm Brandon Clark."

The woman—Jill, if he remembered correctly—blinked rapidly several times, her smooth, creamy complexion coloring the tiniest bit.

Brandon drew his eyebrows together. Why was she acting so surprised? He resisted the urge to check if he had something disgusting stuck to his face.

Before he could confirm or deny that fear, she smoothed her cream-colored sweater down and spoke. "Uh…yes, yes, of course. I'm Jill Lindstrom, Zoe's mother." She took his proffered hand in her much smaller, smoother one, sending tiny streaks of warmth up his arm, taking him off guard. When was the last time *that* had happened?

"Please, come in," she said, quickly pulling her hand from his and gesturing him into the house. She turned to Kristy, standing with Zoe in the foyer.

Both girls were looking back and forth between him and Jill, expectant looks on their faces. Oh, man…

"Hey, Kristy," Jill said, waving. "Glad you two could make it."

Kristy smiled eagerly. "Hi, Mrs. Lindstrom." She

looked at Zoe and let out a silly laugh, shifting her weight from foot to foot.

Brandon raised one brow. Kristy definitely looked as if she had a big, juicy secret. The suspicions he'd had about Kristy and Zoe's motives for this dinner flared again, setting him on a slight edge. Even though Kristy had sworn she and Zoe just wanted him to meet Jill for no particular reason at all, he smelled a major setup. Especially now that he'd seen her.

He tried not to let that unfortunate information bother him, even though anything remotely romantic coming of tonight's dinner was impossible. No way was he going to start down a road that might set him up to lose someone he loved again. Not after Sandy had been taken away from him in such a lingering, heart-ripping way. Not even a gorgeous, family sort of woman like Jill could sway him from that vow.

Zoe gestured in the direction of a small hallway to the rear of the entryway. "You two go on into the kitchen and talk," Zoe said as if she were an adult talking to kids instead of vice versa. "We'll be upstairs." She and Kristy took off up the stairs, giggling the whole way.

Brandon watched them go, shaking his head. "I think we have a couple of matchmakers on our hands," he said to Jill, following her down the hallway. The smell of either lasagna or spaghetti and what he pegged as garlic bread filled the air, making his mouth water.

And yearn for what he used to have. Dinners in a warm kitchen with a woman he loved. Cleaning up together afterward. Cuddling on the couch later and watching TV. Heading upstairs to bed…

Jill turned around when she hit the quaint kitchen, which had oak cabinets and blue-and-white checked curtains. She spread her glossy-looking lips into a big smile. "You figured that out, too?"

He nodded, shoving thoughts of another time, another life far away where they wouldn't bother him quite so much. "Hope you like red." He handed Jill the wine, relieved that it didn't seem as if she was in on the whole matchmaking scheme.

"Love it, and it will go perfectly with the lasagna." She set the wine on the counter, then moved to the cupboard. "Good choice."

"But not exactly lucky," he said, noting how Jill's wavy, shoulder-length hair color was an unusual combination of honey-gold and wheat-colored blond he really liked. Was it as soft as it looked? "Kristy has been talking of nothing but this dinner for days. I was constantly updated about the menu possibilities, so red wine was a no-brainer."

"Ah, I see. I'll just get a couple of wineglasses out, along with the garlic bread in the oven, and then we can eat." She gestured to a wooden stool at a small eating bar on the other side of the Formica counter. "Have a seat for a minute."

Brandon sat, propping his forearms on the edge of the counter. "So you suspected the girls' motives, too?"

"It didn't take too much to figure it out," Jill said, setting two wineglasses on the counter. She then moved to the oven, picking up an oven mitt along the way. "Zoe was pretty obvious and very persistent." Bending, she opened the oven and checked the foil-covered loaf of garlic bread.

Brandon rubbed his jaw, doing his best not to stare at the nice view of Jill's rear end, but failing. Man, she looked good in those jeans. "Hmm. Must have been planned down to a T. Kristy told me what to wear and asked me if I'd brushed my teeth before we left." He let out a rueful laugh, impressed by the girls' planning. "I'm sure she would have hit me with some aftershave if she'd thought of it."

Jill straightened, the bread in her hand. "I agree they've manipulated us into this evening for their own ridiculous purposes." She looked at him, a hint of regret shining in her pretty eyes. "I hope you don't mind too much."

He shook his head. "Nope. I agreed to this because I wanted to spend more time with Kristy and because Zoe is the only friend Kristy has made since we moved to Elm Corners two months ago. I'm not about to squash her enthusiasm for their friendship."

He didn't add that he was ecstatic that Kristy seemed to be happy for the first time in forever. He prayed she settled into small-town life and that their relationship would grow stronger now that he'd ditched his job as a corporate attorney with killer hours in favor of opening a restaurant so he could spend more time with Kristy. Being a restaurateur was in his blood; he'd grown up in the business in Seattle, watching his father run two successful fine dining establishments with his brother.

Brandon loved his daughter more than life itself, and was determined to raise her right, despite having to do it alone. Even though he would still be working a lot of hours, especially until he hired a manager, Kristy could spend time with him at the restaurant after school. He was his own boss now, a blessing he planned to take advantage of to build a closer relationship with his daughter.

"Well, Zoe seems fond of Kristy, too," Jill said, putting the bread on a cutting board. "It's like they've been friends forever." She made quick work of the bread, cutting it into thick slices and setting it in a cloth-lined wicker basket.

"Anything I can do?" Brandon asked, feeling as if he needed to do something besides just show up and eat.

"You could pour the wine. I'll have Zoe pour her and Kristy's drinks."

Brandon opened the wine and poured it, then took both glasses and the bottle to the dining-room table, set with casual stoneware and utensils with chunky metal handles. Jill brought the bread in and called the girls.

A few minutes later Zoe and Kristy bounded into the dining room, their faces awash in speculative looks. Zoe poured them their drinks—grape soda pop, a special treat—and then all four of them sat down to eat.

Jill served everyone lasagna, which looked delicious, and Caesar salad covered in Parmesan cheese and croutons. Kristy started the bread around the table, and Brandon served himself a big slice.

Before he could dig in to his meal, Zoe piped up with, "Hey, Mr. Clark, did you know my mom belongs to The Health Hut?" She gave him an eager grin. "Don't you work out all the time?"

Brandon gave her an indulgent smile. Nine-year-old girls certainly weren't very subtle. "Actually, Zoe, I do. I've been running since we moved here because I haven't had time to join a gym." He turned his attention to Jill. "What do you think of The Health Hut?"

She lifted one slim shoulder. "I think it's the only gym in Elm Corners, so I like it."

"Maybe you should join, Mr. Clark," Zoe suggested, her eyes alight with enthusiasm. "You two could work out together."

While the thought of Jill Lindstrom in workout gear sounded great—he was pretty sure she'd have great legs—Brandon wouldn't ever spend any personal time with her; dating definitely wasn't on his to-do list. "I don't know," he said, attempting to sound noncommittal. It wouldn't be fair to get the girls' hopes up.

His tactic rolled right off Zoe, who looked at her mom and said, "Mom, you should take him to the gym with you tomorrow and help him find out about a membership."

Jill glanced at Zoe, then took a healthy swig of wine. "I'm certainly willing to show him around the Hut if he wants me to, but it's up to him." She turned her attention his way, her mouth curved into a tight smile that seemed to say, *Humor them and they'll lay off.*

He liked her style, and her idea. "I'll get back to you on that, okay?"

"Okay," Jill said, pushing her hair behind one ear. "I go three times a week after Zoe goes to school."

He nodded but didn't reply, eating instead. Man, she was pretty, and nice, too. Very, very appealing in a lot of ways. Honestly, he kind of wanted to take her up on her offer and hang out at the gym with her. Just the thought of Jill in shorts and a T-shirt turned him on.

Whoa. Spending any personal time with Jill, especially any time that exposed her long, lean legs was a bad, bad idea, one that he was sure sounded so damn good only because he'd been without any serious female companionship for so long. A necessary evil he ruthlessly enforced to protect himself and Kristy from hurt.

He had to remember that. Though surprisingly he regretted it, Jill had to remain nothing more than his daughter's best friend's mother.

After a lively discussion about the girls' school, an amusing story about Kristy's kitty, Beau, and Jill's advice to Brandon about the best place to have his dress shirts dry-cleaned, Zoe and Kristy popped up from their seats, grabbed their plates and hightailed it out of the dining room. Zoe, the crafty little manipulator, dimmed the dining-room lights on the way into the kitchen, leaving Jill alone with Brandon in the slightly darkened room.

Jill suppressed an amused yet wary smile and finished off her glass of wine. Before she could start the conversation back up, flowery instrumental music floated in from the stereo in the family room. Apparently the girls were setting the mood.

A shiver of anxiety shot through Jill. She deftly avoided Brandon's hot, dark gaze, forcing herself to relax, even though sitting in a darkened room with a good-looking man she'd just met, music wafting through the air, wasn't exactly relaxing.

She shoved that thought aside. She was in charge of her romantic destiny, no matter what kind of corny, contrived romantic situations Zoe and Kristy cooked up.

"They're not terribly subtle, are they?" Brandon said over his wineglass, his dark eyes twinkling.

Jill shook her head. "No, they're not," she said.

"Next thing you know they'll be herding us to a church to get married."

While she liked the fact that Brandon could joke about a situation that could be construed as embarrassing and awkward, a flash of guilt shot through her. "I'm…sorry for all of this. I knew they were up to something, but I had no idea how far they'd take it."

He put down his empty wineglass, holding up a

hand. "Don't worry about it. I think it's kind of endearing, and I have to admire the lengths they've gone to to make this work. They've really put some thought into all of this."

Jill's face warmed. "I'm afraid we have my daughter to thank for most of it. She's quite determined, and I'm pretty sure she had some outside help."

He raised his eyebrows in an unspoken question.

Jill sighed. "My dad spends a lot of time with Zoe, and he's...well, he's an inventor of sorts, and Zoe is really into the whole inventing thing." Jill accepted that situation because of the good relationship Zoe and her grandpa had. But deep down, it bothered Jill that her daughter was so keen on following in "Wacky" Winters's footsteps, a path that had been a burden to Jill her whole life.

"So...what?" Brandon threw her a quizzical look. "You think they're trying to invent a mom and dad by having you and me get together?"

"Pretty much."

Brandon laughed, a deep rich sound that made goose bumps scatter across Jill's skin. "Well, I have to hand it to them. They've done an amazing job." He hit her with a crooked grin, his eyes intent on her face, setting off a hot shiver. "If I were in the market for a romance, I'd hire them."

Jill quickly looked at her plate, ignoring how his simple look lit fires inside her, choosing instead to focus on how much she wanted to ask Brandon why he was so obviously *not* in the market for a romance.

But she held back. That was too personal a question to ask a man she'd just met, even if he did light up her senses and turn her dormant libido back on.

She focused instead on how she appreciated that he was being such a good sport about their scheming daughters. She sneaked a glance at him, also really liking his dark good looks, charming sense of humor and knee-weakening smile.

Before she could go very far with that thought, a loud explosion sounded from out back, rattling the silverware on the table.

Her face heating—darn her dad's timing—Jill quickly glanced at Brandon, noting with little surprise that his dark eyes were wide with shock.

"What was that?" Brandon asked.

"Oh, don't worry," she said, casually waving a hand in the air, hoping to minimize the whole embarrassing event. "It's just my dad…inventing in his workshop out back."

She fiddled with her napkin, praying her dad didn't follow his usual routine and come inside. The last thing she wanted was for Brandon to meet her eccentric father—many people reacted to his goofy looks with disbelieving laughter—although why she cared at all what Brandon thought was a mystery.

Brandon smiled, his dark eyes twinkling. "Ah, good. I thought maybe an airliner had crashed in the backyard."

Jill let out a sigh, wishing she could appreciate his joke. "No, no, nothing as dramatic as that. Just my dad doing his thing." The thing that had set her apart from everybody when she'd been growing up. How many times had other kids teased her because of her dad's crazy invention antics, chanting "Wacky Winters is so weird," over and over again? How many times had someone in town laughingly asked how Wacky was, a question that was always followed by something like "Has he blown up anything important yet?"

Right on schedule, she heard the back door open and close. "Jilly," her dad called. "You here?"

Jill rolled her eyes. Oh, brother. Her dad knew darn well she was here, since he'd undoubtedly been in on the girls' matchmaking plan. "Yes, Dad," she replied, resigned to the inevitable introductions—and Brandon's amusement. "In the dining room."

A moment later her dad burst through the door into the dining room, his wild gray curly hair sticking out at all angles, his black horn-rimmed glasses—held together with duct tape—askew. Every inch of his six-foot-two-inch frame was covered in black soot and bits of what looked like…bright pink silly string? What in the world had he been doing this time?

He straightened his glasses and smoothed his hair, which didn't make his kinky hair smooth at all. It just made the top flat and the bottom fluffier. "Sorry for the noise. Just wanted to let you know I'm fine." His blue eyes caught on Brandon. "Hey, Brandon. Good to see you here."

Jill pulled in her chin. "You two know each other?"

Brandon nodded and stood. "We met picking the girls up from their Girl Scout meetings." He thrust out his hand, looking pleased to see her dad again, not a trace of laughter popping from his mouth. "Good to see you, Wacky."

Her dad wiped his hand on his pants and shook Brandon's hand. "You, too, Brandon." He looked at Jill. "I'm not going to interrupt you two anymore, Jilly." He wagged his eyebrows suggestively, a sure sign he'd had a hand in inviting Brandon here this evening. "Gotta go clean up. Send the girls out so I can show them my latest project." Ever since she was big enough, Zoe had been her grandpa's assistant; she spent hours hanging out in his lab with him, working on his various projects. She'd become quite the little inventor in her own right. Jill only hoped Zoe would eventually find other interests.

With that, Jill's dad left the dining room, a long length of toilet paper stuck to the bottom of one shoe.

Jill snorted under her breath. *Really attractive, Dad.*

Her cheeks fired up again. She fought the desire to drop her head into her hands and scream out her frustration and embarrassment. Not only was she sure her dad had helped the girls with their scheme, acting on his intense but futile desire to see her married again, but he'd pranced into the dining room in his full mad-scientist glory, toilet paper of all things trailing behind him.

Would he never stop embarrassing her?

She mentally noted the need to have a very frank discussion with her dad right away. She knew from experience that nothing she could say would change his wacky personality; his nickname was disgustingly appropriate. But she would darn sure give him a piece of her mind for egging the girls on in the matchmaking department.

Taking a deep breath, she reined in her spiraling emotions. She looked at Brandon, keeping her face deliberately neutral, hoping to downplay her father's strange behavior. "Sorry about that. I was hoping there wouldn't be any explosions tonight."

Brandon grinned and sat back down. "Don't be sorry. I like him. He's an original."

Jill relaxed a bit, loving the fact that he didn't seem to think her dad was anything unusual. Or if he did, he was graciously keeping that unfortunate information to himself. "That's putting it mildly."

"So, does he live with you?" Brandon asked.

Jill cleared her throat. "Kind of. He has an apartment above his laboratory out back." Jill hadn't really wanted to live with her dad when she'd moved back to Elm Corners after Doug had left her. After living with her dad's madcap ways her whole childhood, his crazy, never-know-what-to-expect lifestyle didn't really appeal to her.

But when he'd suggested she move in to the house, announcing he wanted to live above his lab out back, she'd taken him up on the offer, needing his help with Zoe. She'd also realized that, considering she didn't have a job when she'd moved, living with him made financial sense. And she had to admit, crazy inventions aside, he was a great grandpa, Zoe adored him and his babysitting help had been invaluable to a single working mom like Jill.

Needing to change the subject from her one-of-a-kind, exasperating dad, she asked Brandon the first question that popped into her head. "So, Brandon. What do you do?" Oh, how she hoped he was in some weird line of work that would cancel out how appealing he was in other ways.

He settled back into his chair. "Well, I was a lawyer when we lived in L.A. But I've dumped all that to start my own business."

"And what kind of business are you starting?" Jill asked, truly interested. For some reason she couldn't put her finger on, Brandon seemed like the kind of guy who would succeed in anything he did.

"I'm opening a restaurant on Main Street. Maybe you've seen the signs." He leaned forward, his eyes full of undisguised excitement and pride. "It's called The Steak Place."

Jill's stomach dropped. No way!

She stared at him to make sure he wasn't goofing around. He sat there looking at her, appearing totally serious.

She pressed her lips together and shifted on her chair. Oh, she'd seen the stupid signs, all right, every time she went to work. Brandon was the person who'd taken the lease for the adjoining space right out from under her nose!

Her cheeks blazed to life. Well, hurray. It looked as if her wish had come true. His line of work *was* unappealing.

He was her competitor, someone who could spell disaster for not only her livelihood, but also her plans to be a successful, well-respected businesswoman.

Put simply, he was a man she wished had never come to town.

Chapter Two

"Your cheeks are all red," Brandon said, his deep voice laced with obvious concern. "What's wrong?"

Jill snapped her gaze to him, her face still blazing, her thoughts racing. Well, la-di-da. Looked as if she was going to be able to drop a bomb of her own. Brandon obviously had no clue that she owned the restaurant next door to his. "Has Kristy told you what *I* do for a living?" she asked.

He drew his eyebrows together. "Uh, well…no, I guess not."

Jill rolled her eyes and let out an under-the-breath snort. Zoe and Kristy hadn't let either of them in on the fact that they were business competitors of the first degree. Wait till she got her hands on Zoe!

"I own The Wildflower Grill, the other restaurant on Main Street," she informed him.

For a moment the truth didn't faze Brandon. Then understanding dawned in his eyes. "Oh," he said. "So we're…competitors."

Jill nodded, roughly rolling the stem of her wineglass between her fingers. "Yes, competitors," she snapped, then instantly regretted her rude tone.

"Is that a problem?" he asked, looking genuinely perplexed. "Granted, I didn't know you owned a restaurant, but it shouldn't be that big of a deal, should it?"

Jill looked at him, trying to figure him out. Was it possible he hadn't known she'd wanted the space between their two businesses? Gene Hobart, the landlord, was a shrewd businessman, and not above being sleazy when it came to snagging the client who would up his profits the most. Had Gene even told Brandon that Jill was interested in the space, or that she'd specifically told Gene she wanted the space when it became available? Or that Gene had unofficially promised to come to her with a deal first?

Maybe Gene was the bad guy here, and not Brandon.

"Maybe," she said, forcing herself to stay calm and rational.

"Why is that? Do you automatically hate other restaurant owners?" he asked, his mouth quirked into a teasing smile that would be so easy to return.

She resisted the urge, reminding herself that he could be a charmer who might like to charm her right into rolling over and going out of business, clearing the way for his business to flourish.

She let out a short, irritated breath. "For one, Mr. Clark, you chose a spot two doors from my restaurant, which certainly doesn't bode well for my business. Secondly, I wanted to lease the vacant space between the two restaurants, and even though Gene promised me first crack, you got it instead." She pressed her lips together and looked right at him, glaring. "Do you know how long I'd saved to be able to afford to lease that space when it became available?"

He didn't respond right away. After a long moment of silence, he leaned forward. "Look," he said, his eyes reflecting a serious light, "for the record, I chose the spot I did because it was the best retail location for my restaurant, which I'm sure you can confirm. You chose the same stretch of property, right on Main Street, where you'd be assured the best return on your investment. You can't fault me for being a good businessman.

"Second, I had no idea you wanted the space next to yours. Gene offered it to me as one space, package deal, end of story."

Jill remained silent, thinking. He'd made some good points, she'd give him that, but his presence in Elm Corners still threatened everything that was important to her careerwise. "How in the world am I supposed to do well with you right next door, literally stealing customers away?" she asked.

"No offense, Jill, but you've had it pretty easy as the only game in town in the way of fine dining."

She crossed her arms over her chest, her pride forcing her to omit what a rough road she'd had building her business, how difficult it had been to convince the staid population of Elm Corners to try a new restaurant. Business was more stable now, but the first year had been very, very lean, and she'd almost had to close The Grill several times. Only through sheer determination, a very understanding, devoted staff and a lot of creative advertising and promotions had she been able to draw in enough customers to stay afloat. Even now, though she was in the black, she was just barely making ends meet. It wouldn't take much of a downturn in business to shove her back in the red. "Which is one of the reasons, I'm sure, that you chose to start a restaurant here."

He tilted his head to the side, then nodded. "Touché. I grew up in the restaurant business, so I knew enough to do some market research before coming here, and, of course, I knew that there was only one other fine-dining establishment in Elm Corners. But that's irrelevant."

"Not to me," she said under her breath, knowing as she said the words that she was being unreasonable. She also knew, however, that anything that threatened her dream of business success would push her buttons and freak her out.

"I'm sorry this is a problem for you," he said, sounding totally sincere. "For what it's worth, I had no idea that you were the owner of the restaurant next door."

She looked at him, wishing he was a jerk so she could really hate him. But he wasn't a jerk. He was a seemingly good guy who just happened to be her only competition. Deal breaker, that. They could never be friends.

She stood. "I believe you, Brandon." Her jaw tight, she began to clear the dinner dishes.

After a long moment, he reached out and grabbed her hand as she reached for a salad bowl. "You're mad at me, aren't you?"

She stilled, liking the feel of his big, warm hand on hers just a little too much. Forcing herself to pull her hand away, she replied, "I'm not mad, really, just…surprised to discover that you're the person I've been cursing up and down for the last week."

He rose and began gathering dishes. "That doesn't sound very good."

"It isn't," Jill replied truthfully. She wasn't going to sugarcoat how worried and frustrated and irritated she was that he'd leased a space for a restaurant in Elm Corners, never mind right next door.

When they reached the kitchen, he set the dishes on the counter. "So, I guess you're not interested in showing me around The Health Hut." He drilled her with those beautiful dark eyes, sending a hot, thrilling chill skating up her spine.

She set her jaw, chasing off the way he could just look at her and make her want to grab him and kiss him silly. "You know, I don't think I'd be much help. Cindy Jones runs the place. She can show you around." The last thing Jill needed to do was actually spend time with the man who could spell disaster for her business goals.

Brandon nodded, his jaw noticeably tight. "Okay, thanks."

Jill began to rinse and load the dinner dishes, and Brandon helped out, even going so far as to gather up the tablecloth and shake it out outside. Darn it, anyway, why did he have to be so nice, so attractive, such an all-around considerate guy?

Big deal. So he was nice. The important thing was that he wasn't her friend or even an acquaintance, just a man her daughter had thrown Jill together with for a ridiculous reason. Now that she'd discovered who he was, she needed him gone, right now. She'd be a masochistic idiot to hang around with the owner of The Steak Place.

"You know," she said, loading the last of the dishes into the dishwasher, "I think I feel a headache coming on."

Brandon paused, a sponge in his hand. "You want me to get you some pain reliever?" He moved closer, his dark eyes full of concern. "Why don't you sit down and I'll finish up here."

Jill bit her lip, wishing he wasn't so solicitous. It would be much easier to dislike him that way, and she really needed to dislike him. "Uh, no, that's okay." She shut the dishwasher. "But I do think we should cut the evening short."

After a long, almost disbelieving silence, he said,

"Of course. I'll go call Kristy." He headed out of the kitchen, leaving Jill alone, feeling like a total fool for allowing the girls to set up this dinner in the first place, although in her defense, she'd had no idea that her dinner guest was the owner of The Steak Place.

Kristy and Zoe came downstairs and whined about the evening ending so soon, especially since they hadn't gone out to Zoe's grandpa's lab yet. But Jill stood firm, needing to regain the equilibrium Brandon had pushed off balance. It was enough she had to deal with him in her business life, a constant worry she could never get rid of. She sure didn't want to have him stirring up her personal life, either, nor did she want to have to deal with her disturbing physical attraction to him.

"Thank you for dinner," Brandon said at the front door, giving her a small, rueful smile. "I enjoyed meeting you."

"You're welcome," Jill said, deliberately ignoring his smile. "Good luck with your…business." She forced herself to be polite.

Brandon raised his eyebrows, then his expression turned speculative. "You know, this isn't all doom and gloom. Maybe there's room in Elm Corners for two successful restaurants."

"I hope so," Jill replied sincerely, even though she doubted it. She'd struggled when she was the only restaurant game in town. Now that Brandon had arrived, who knew how she was going to survive.

They said goodbye, and Jill watched father and daughter climb into their SUV at the curb and drive away. She turned and went back into the house, rubbing her eyes, her mood darkening when Zoe was nowhere to be found on the main floor. Jill rolled her eyes, her patience wearing thin. Zoe was undoubtedly pouting in her room because the evening hadn't gone as she'd planned.

Jill laughed under her breath without humor. Honestly. What did the girls expect? That she and Brandon would lay eyes on each other one minute and elope the next? Fat chance. Real life just didn't work that way.

Especially since Zoe was manipulating her, shoving her into unwanted situations, hooking her up with a man on the sly. Worse yet, that man had turned out be Jill's archrival, a man who could spell disaster for her restaurant.

No doubt about it. Too many things about this evening had gone all wrong.

Unfortunately, the day was going to get worse. It was time to talk to her stubborn, determined daughter and tell her that things had gone too far and to cool her eager little matchmaking jets.

For good.

"So what did you think of Mrs. Lindstrom?" Kristy asked Brandon the second he pulled away from the curb.

"I thought she was very nice," Brandon replied,

leaving out that he also thought she was downright beautiful, smart and attractive in every way and that in another life he'd love to date her. *Another life* being the key phrase there.

In this life she was his competition, the owner of the business he planned on leaving in the dust. Not exactly dating material.

"Just nice?" Kristy asked, her voice full of eager hope. "I think she's really cool, and pretty, too. And she's a really good cook, don't you think?"

The raw, undisguised hope in his daughter's voice broke Brandon's heart. He knew how much Kristy missed having a mother and how appealing it must be to her to fantasize about having Zoe for a sister. But this wasn't a game, this was real life, and feelings and emotions were at stake. He wasn't going to let himself get sucked into Jill's life, and vice versa, just to make his daughter's far-fetched dreams of a perfect family come true.

Obviously it was time to set the record straight with Kristy. He hated to burst her bubble, but he had to let her know that her matchmaking was futile. "Listen, Kris," he said, stopping at a red light, "I appreciate what you and Zoe are trying to do, but I have to ask you to stop."

"What do you mean?" Kristy asked, her voice monotone. "We're not trying to do anything, Dad."

He smiled, put the car into motion again, then took a quick right turn. Kristy was a terrible liar, which he considered a good thing. "Oh, come on. I might be a little rusty in the dating department, but it doesn't take a genius to figure out that you and Zoe set up the whole evening to get me and Jill together."

Kristy was silent for a long moment. "Would it be so bad if you two liked each other?" she asked, her voice very small.

Oh, man, he hated having to disappoint Kristy. But he had no other choice. She had to understand that a relationship between him and Jill was impossible for way too many reasons. Reasons that now went far beyond his desire to protect his heart.

"Not bad, honey, just not in the cards."

"Why?"

She'd asked a good question, one he'd asked himself many times before, especially in the deep of the night when he felt so alone, so isolated, so empty that he would die for the feel of a woman in his arms once more. The answer was always the same; he simply couldn't put himself in a position to care about a woman again. The risk was just too great, for both him and Kristy.

But he couldn't explain that to her in a way she would understand. She was too young, too stuffed full of girlish romantic dreams to fully grasp what he meant. So he simply said, "Because I don't want to date Jill. She seems like a wonderful woman, but I'm not interested." He knew that sounded kind of harsh, but it was necessary here. The matchmaking had to stop.

Kristy didn't say anything, and Brandon let her keep her silence. She was stewing, which was her way of sorting things out in her own mind. He remained silent, too, hoping she'd eventually understand what he'd said enough to forget about him and Jill getting together. Maybe they'd face each other again in the business arena, but not in any kind of personal way.

As he pulled into his driveway, he had to admit that as they'd been sitting in the dining room sharing a delicious meal, spending some personal time with Jill had appealed to him. Stupid idea, not somewhere he wanted to go, even though she was the sexiest thing he'd seen in a long time.

Thankfully, the discovery of their roles as business competitors had brought him to his senses, and had certainly lit a fire under Jill. Once she'd found out that he was the owner of The Steak Place, she hadn't been able to get rid of him fast enough. Headache, my foot.

Even though the red-blooded male in him regretted he wouldn't be getting to know her on some kind of personal level, keeping his distance was best.

Even if that disappointed Kristy.

"Zoe," Jill yelled over the music coming from Zoe's room. "We have to talk."

While Jill waited for Zoe to answer the door, she reiterated in her mind how important this conversation was. She had to make Zoe understand that any kind of relationship between Jill and Brandon was impossible.

Zoe turned down the music and answered the door, her mouth pulled into a pouty frown. She crossed her arms over her chest and remained silent, her eyes boring holes in Jill.

Regret burned through her. It wasn't easy shooting down her daughter's dreams of a complete family, no matter how unrealistic they were.

She reached out and smoothed the lines between Zoe's eyebrows. "Oh, come on, honey. It's not that bad."

Zoe stomped away and flung herself on her twin bed. "You practically threw them out."

Jill cringed inside, regretting the tactless way she'd hustled the Clarks out the door. "Well…yes, I guess I did hurry them out before I really needed to. But I did it because it was pretty obvious why you and Kristy arranged the dinner. It isn't going to happen."

"Why not?" Zoe asked, her voice full of hope. "Don't you like him?"

The hope in Zoe's voice reminded Jill how much Zoe wanted a whole family. A familiar arrow of guilt tinged with more regret shot through Jill, poking a wounded spot on her heart that had never really healed. Zoe had been deeply affected emotionally by her parents' divorce, something Jill agonized about on a daily basis. Oh, how she wished she could somehow magically obliterate Zoe's pain.

But after a lot of soul-searching over the years, Jill had come to terms with the fact that as long as she was the best mom she could be, Zoe would be just fine, even without a live-in dad. She would provide unlimited, unconditional love and support to her daughter, no matter what.

But she wasn't a magician, and one thing she couldn't do was wave a wand and provide an instant family for Zoe. That was an impossible dream that was not going to come true, and it would save Zoe a lot of heartache and fallen hopes if she understood that now.

"He's very…charming," Jill said, telling the truth even as she needed to make sure Zoe understood that her thinking a man was charming didn't mean love and happily ever after were just around the corner. "But…well, Zoe, I'm not interested in a romantic relationship."

She hoped Zoe would accept that fact and move on. At nine, Zoe certainly wouldn't understand Jill's deep-seated need to protect herself from being dumped again. Especially since Jill really didn't want to trash Doug to Zoe. While Zoe didn't see her dad very often, they spent enough time together that Jill would never risk ruining their fragile bond by criticizing Doug.

"Don't you want to fall in love again?" Zoe asked with all the innocence and hope of a naive, stars-in-her-eyes young girl who, of course, had never had her heart ripped out by someone who was supposed to love and cherish her for all time.

Jill hesitated, formulating an answer that would appease Zoe's curiosity without Jill having to try to explain how down on love she was—and why. She'd never shared those feelings with anyone. "Love isn't something I crave like I used to," she said, basically speaking the truth, although there were times when she missed the companionship and closeness inherent in a romantic relationship. "I'd rather focus on my business than on trying to find a boyfriend." At least her business would stick by her instead of deserting her, leaving her heartbroken and aching.

Zoe looked at her, her blue eyes full of doubt. "Oh, come on, Mom. You can't tell me that the restaurant is going to take the place of love." She rolled her eyes. "That's just dumb."

Dumb, maybe, but safe. "The point, honey, is that I'm just not interested in Brandon, especially since he owns The Steak Place, and I need you to stop trying to get us together. I'll have a talk with your grandpa and tell him, too."

"Does it really matter that much that Mr. Clark has a restaurant, too?"

"Yes, it does," Jill replied, fully believing her own words. "You know how hard I've worked to make The Grill successful." She'd leave it at that, deliberately vague. The last thing she wanted to do was share the gory details of her financial worries with her daughter. No child should have to worry about something like that.

Zoe looked at her for a long moment, chewing on her lip, a sure sign the wheels were spinning in her brain. Then she let out a long sigh and picked up a Harry Potter book. "Whatever you say," she said in a manufactured tone that told Jill that Zoe was going to ignore every single thing Jill had told her. "I've got reading to do."

"So you understand that the matchmaking has to stop, right?" Jill asked, needing Zoe to speak the words to convince Jill she'd back off.

"Sure, Mom," Zoe said, smiling brightly. Too brightly. "I get it, okay?"

Jill stared at her daughter, her eyes narrowed. Zoe seemed to be taking all of this really well, and that raised a huge red flag. She knew her daughter well enough to know when Zoe was placating her so she could ambush her down the line. Zoe was nothing if not stubborn.

Weary of the whole thing, Jill decided not to push the issue anymore tonight. She would have plenty of time to get her point across to Zoe tomorrow. And the next day. And the day after that.

"Okay." She stepped back and gently pulled the door closed behind her, feeling a real headache coming on.

Great. A headache to match the tight, burning knot of frustration and anxiety that was taking up what she suspected would be permanent residence in her chest.

Because no matter what Zoe had said, no matter how accepting of the situation she seemed to be, Jill was pretty sure that her stubborn, determined daughter wasn't going to back off at all. Oh, no. She definitely had more up her sleeve.

Unfortunately, Jill's troubles with Brandon Clark weren't going to go away any time soon. Because this matchmaking invention of Zoe and Kristy's wasn't over.

Not by a long shot.

Chapter Three

The day after he'd had dinner with the Lindstroms, Brandon stepped into Elm Corners Elementary School's tiny front office. He wasn't that surprised to see Jill sitting in one of the shabby upholstered chairs pushed against one wall.

She wore a slim pair of jeans and a form-fitting pink sweater that showed off all her curves just right. To add to her appeal, she had her golden hair pulled back in a sleek ponytail that highlighted the fine bone structure of her face, her flawless complexion and striking blue eyes.

Without warning, his heart rate kicked up a notch, fueling his insane desire to step close and turn her face up for a kiss.

She turned and looked at him and a wary smile

followed. Right on cue, he found it hard to breathe, even though her expression told him she wasn't thrilled to see the man she viewed as the Big Bad Restaurant Owner who was going to leave her penniless.

"Jill," he managed to say, despite his shortness of breath. "Why am I not surprised to see you here?"

She stood, smoothing her already perfect hair back with one hand. "Zoe was caught fighting. I'm guessing Kristy was, too?"

Brandon nodded curtly, hot irritation burning through him. "You got it. I can't believe she didn't listen to one thing I told her last night." Because of the girls' determination to get him and Jill together, and because of how close Zoe and Kristy were, his gut instincts told him that the "fight" had been a ploy, rather than the real thing. Besides, Kristy didn't have a violent bone in her body, and neither, he suspected, did Zoe.

Jill hitched her purse up onto her shoulder with a jerk. "Yes, well, I can believe it. Zoe pretended— badly, I might add—to cooperate, but I was pretty sure it wasn't going to be that easy to get her to back off."

"Apparently I underestimated their persistence." He shook his head, feeling the fool for believing that the girls would let this whole matchmaking thing drop without a fight. "Tactical error."

"Mr. Clark? Mrs. Lindstrom?" Mrs. Jacobs, the middle-aged principal, said from her office door. "I can see you now."

Brandon followed Jill into the drab, windowless

office, its only saving grace the numerous colorful children's drawings taped to the wall. He sat next to Jill in a chair facing the principal's desk, preparing for the worst.

Mrs. Jacobs didn't waste any time delivering the bad news. Her green eyes serious, she said, "Mrs. Lindstrom, Mr. Clark, Kristy and Zoe were caught fighting with each other on the playground at recess earlier today."

"They were fighting...with each other?" Jill asked, her voice rife with disbelief, taking the words right out of Brandon's mouth. While he'd known Kristy had been caught fighting and had deduced the fight had been staged to bring him and Jill together, he was stunned that the girls had actually become violent with each other.

Mrs. Jacobs nodded. "I thought that was strange, too, since they've become such good friends. But apparently they had a falling out. The teacher on playground duty, Mrs. Sanderson, caught them right after lunch. They were actually rolling around on the grass, pulling each other's hair."

Brandon released a heavy breath, floored that Kristy would take their scheme this far. "Have you talked to the girls?" he asked.

Mrs. Jacobs nodded. "Yes, I have, and both of them said they were fighting about a Barbie Kristy borrowed and hadn't returned. It sounded like a lame excuse, especially for two such well-behaved girls, but that's all they would say."

Jill rolled her eyes in obvious annoyance, then cleared her throat and spoke up again. "This isn't about Barbie dolls," she said, shaking her head. "Zoe and Kristy adore each other, and wouldn't fight for real over toys. The thing is, Mrs. Jacobs, the girls have been trying to…" She turned and looked at Brandon. "How should I put it?"

Brandon took over. "Put bluntly, they've been trying to…create a romantic relationship between Mrs. Lindstrom and myself."

Mrs. Jacobs's eyebrows disappeared into her hairline. "Ah. I see. So you think this was just a ploy to get the two of you together?"

He and Jill nodded simultaneously, and Jill said, "Precisely. And it worked, didn't it? Here we are, doing exactly what they want."

Mrs. Jacobs folded her hands on her desk. "Yes, it seems so, although that doesn't give me license to condone their behavior."

"And we're not asking you to," Brandon said, belatedly realizing his use of the word *we* made him and Jill sound like a couple. "*I* felt you should hear a likely explanation for the girls' behavior." He leaned forward, determined to be the kind of father Kristy needed—one who wouldn't let this little act go unpunished. "What's the usual punishment for fighting?"

"Manners School on the first offense," Mrs. Jacobs informed him. "They will be required to stay after school for the next three days and clean their teachers' rooms."

A little manual labor sounded good to Brandon. Anything to knock some sense into his daughter and nip her unacceptable behavior in the proverbial bud. "Perfect. And you can be assured Kristy will receive additional punishment and a long lecture from me."

"I plan on doing the same with Zoe," Jill said. "Fighting is fighting, no matter the reason."

"Excellent," Mrs. Jacobs said. "I would hate to see two such wonderful girls stuck in Manners School for very long."

Everyone rose, then Brandon preceded Jill out the door into the front office. After they said goodbye and thank you to Mrs. Jacobs, he followed Jill to the parking lot, remaining silent, stewing on his own thoughts. Kristy had crossed a line, and that troubled him deeply.

Jill reached her car and stopped, looking at him with outright annoyance shining in her ocean-colored eyes. "They've done it again, haven't they?"

He nodded, sharing her irritation, trying not to stare too much at her lovely face at a time when their kids were causing so much trouble. "Yes, they have, even after I told Kristy in no uncertain terms to stop."

"I had the same conversation with Zoe," Jill said, shaking her head, a rueful smile forming on her lips. "They totally blew us off."

Brandon couldn't resist returning her cute smile, feeling his tension ease a bit. "They're obviously more determined than we thought."

He remained silent, chewing on the inside of his

mouth as an idea formulated in his head. "Listen, I think we need to talk about this," he finally said. "You up for coffee?"

Jill raised a delicately arched, dark blond brow. "Wouldn't that be playing right into their hands?"

"Well…yes," he conceded. "But we can't let this whole thing get out of control, can we?" He was just being smart here, trying to resolve a mutual problem with Jill before the girls got totally out of hand. "I promise, it won't be a date. I'll even let you buy your own coffee if it makes you feel better."

She remained silent for a long moment, nibbling on her glossy pink lower lip in a way that made him want to be the one doing the nibbling.

"All right," she finally said. "Coffee is fine, but it's only because we really have to talk about how to handle Zoe and Kristy. And I can't stay too long." She looked at her watch. "It's Friday, one of The Grill's biggest nights, and I have to get back to work."

"Fine by me," he said, understanding her need to return to The Grill. It wouldn't be long before he'd have a Friday-night dinner crowd to deal with, too. "I have a meeting at three."

They agreed to meet in neutral territory on Main Street at Coffee Crazy, Elm Corner's attempt at coffee chic.

As he drove to the center of town, Brandon gripped the steering wheel, his thoughts somber. Kristy had gone a long way to invent herself a whole family.

A burning lump of regret and sadness settled in the center of his chest. Of course Kristy really missed having a mom. She was shy, too, and friendships were hard for her to form; moving to a new school hadn't been easy. Her new best friend would make the most awesome sister in the whole world. All good reasons for her to want her plan to work.

But Zoe and Kristy's matchmaking scheme couldn't be successful. While he would lay down his life for her and move heaven and earth to make sure she was safe and happy, jumping into a relationship with Jill—or any woman—just to make his daughter's world right would be foolish.

No, that just wasn't something he could allow himself to do.

While he hated to cut Kristy's dreams down, the sooner she understood that he and Jill were never going to be an item, the better.

Jill sat at a corner table at Coffee Crazy and watched Brandon order their coffee at the front counter, his tall, broad-shouldered frame dwarfing most of the other patrons. A tingle of feminine appreciation shot through her, warming her from the inside out.

She made herself ignore that Brandon was one drop-dead-handsome guy. Taking a deep breath, she forced her fluttery nerves into submission.

Get a grip. So he was the most attractive man she'd met in aeons. So she'd been fantasizing about what it would be like to kiss him—a lot. So she'd like to stick pins in a voodoo doll that looked like him, given that he was the owner of The Steak Place. She was an adult, perfectly capable of having a rational discussion, no matter what the circumstance. She'd simply drink her coffee, discuss the girls and that would be that.

Feeling marginally calmer, she smoothed a stray strand of hair back, focusing on her headstrong daughter.

Outright exasperation started bubbling inside her all over again. Darn Zoe, anyway. However, Jill wasn't at all surprised that Zoe hadn't listened to her about stopping her attempts to get her and Brandon together. When Zoe decided to do something, there was no stopping her. Add Jill's father's influence into the mix and she had one impossible situation on her hands.

Nevertheless, this scheme of Zoe and Kristy's had to stop. Next thing she knew, Brandon would be miraculously showing up every time she turned around thanks to the naive romantic fantasies of two young girls.

She suppressed a shudder. No, she didn't want to deal with Brandon at all. If she had to drive him out of business, well, fine. Great, in fact. But she had to make sure Mr. Steak Place stayed out of her personal life permanently.

Brandon headed to the table, two large coffees in his hands. In a pair of khakis and a cream-colored, button-down oxford shirt he looked good enough to eat. His black leather coat contrasted perfectly with his chestnut-shaded hair and olive complexion and made his dark eyes look like ebony velvet.

Jill forced herself to set aside how yummy he looked, attributing her notice of his good looks to the fact that she hadn't been in a social situation alone with a man since the Ice Age.

He arrived at the table and set both cups of coffee down. He then lowered himself into the chair across the small table from Jill, inadvertently, she was sure, pushing his large knees against hers.

Jill's stomach dipped and her heart bounced at the contact. Right on cue, tiny hot fires flared to life inside. She discreetly tried to move back, wishing she'd chosen a bigger table.

She picked up her decaf coffee. "Thanks." She took a large sip of the strong, fragrant brew, hoping it calmed her jittery nerves.

He took a sip of coffee, his dark gaze sticking on her over his cup. "So, what are we going to do about the girls?"

She shook her head, warming her hands on her coffee cup. "I have no idea. Obviously just talking to them isn't going to work."

Brandon shifted in his chair, looking vaguely uneasy. "Listen," he said after a long, awkward silence, "I think we need to be totally honest to find a solution to this problem."

"I agree." And she did. To a point.

"Okay," he said, putting his coffee down. "Then first we need to discuss exactly why Kristy and Zoe are so gung ho to get us together."

"I think that's pretty obvious," Jill said. "Zoe wants a dad and Kristy wants a mom, not to mention how cool they must think it would be to be sisters."

"You've got that right." Brandon scrubbed a hand across his face. "Lately Kristy has become obsessed with nail polish, clothes and shopping, none of which are exactly my forte."

A tight knot of sympathy for Kristy—and Brandon—formed in Jill's throat. "You know, Zoe and I go shopping all the time. I'd be happy to include Kristy."

"I admire that you can set aside our…business issues to help Kristy out," Brandon said, pinning her in place with those dark, sexy eyes of his.

She swallowed, her heart racing at his stare, and looked down at her coffee cup. "I know how hard it is as a girl to grow up without a mom, and it's hardly Kristy's fault you moved your restaurant in next door to mine. I'd be happy to help out with her any way I can."

"I appreciate that." He fiddled with a sugar packet on the table. "So what about Zoe? Why is she so anxious for us to get together?"

Jill tilted her head to the side, thinking. "You know, that's a good question. She has my dad, and she sees her own dad every so often, so I don't think it's all about having a father figure in her life, although I'm sure that's a part of it."

"What's the rest?"

Jill drew in a deep breath. "Honestly, I think it's more her dreams of the perfect family that are driving a lot of this. And maybe her girlish fantasies about how neat it would be for not only her mom to be swept off her feet and fall madly in love, but to get a built-in sister who happens to be her best friend in the deal."

"That does sound pretty tempting, doesn't it?" Brandon asked with a nod.

"Yes, I guess it does—not that those reasons change anything," she said. No matter how good the motivation for Zoe's crazy scheme, Jill still couldn't let her daughter manipulate her.

"So now that we've established their motivation, let's discuss why their scheme won't work," he said.

Jill pulled in her chin, frowning. "It just won't."

"Why, exactly?" he asked, leaning closer. "We need ammunition, Jill."

Their business relationship was established. He had to be talking about any possible *personal* reasons that the girls' plan wouldn't work.

She sighed heavily, her stomach twisting. Sharing her deepest feelings about how she wanted to avoid putting her heart on the line, and why, would be difficult. Especially since she wanted to keep their relationship impersonal.

"We're direct competitors," she said, going with the obvious in hopes he would leave the conversation at that.

"Yes, we are. But technically that shouldn't stop us from being involved personally, right?"

"Wrong," she said, holding up a hand, palm out. "Don't you think it would be a little weird for you to be dating the competition?" She arched her brows. "Talk about a conflict of interest."

He raised his hands in the air. "Okay, okay, I see your point. But I still think we need more ammunition than that, especially since we're dealing with two young girls who don't know the meaning of conflict of interest and still believe that Barbie and Ken are the perfect couple."

He had a good point. "Why don't you start, then?" she asked, smiling sweetly. Let him be the guinea pig and spill his guts first.

He tilted his head to the side, a gleam of what looked like admiration in his eyes. "Turning the tables, right?"

She nodded tersely. "You bet."

"Fine. I'll go first." He took another sip of coffee, a shadow slowly growing in his eyes. "I'm sure you know that I'm a widower."

She nodded, her chest tightening. She regretted a bit that she was forcing him to discuss something so painful, even though this honesty business was his idea. "Yes. Zoe told me that. I'm so sorry."

"Thank you." He swallowed. "Well, when Sandy died, I was devastated, even though I had plenty of time to prepare for it." He set his jaw, keeping his eyes on the table. "The cancer took a long time to get her."

Oh, no, no, no. Jill's eyes stung.

Brandon continued, shifting his gaze to his coffee cup, but not fast enough that she didn't see the lingering sadness in his eyes. "Losing her was the worst thing that has ever happened to me. It simply hurt too damn much for me to ever willingly put myself in a position to experience that again."

Jill fought off tears, feeling his pain deep in her soul. "So that's why you don't want a relationship with me?"

"With you or any woman," he said resolutely, "so don't be offended. Honestly, though, I think I could get around the business competitor thing if I didn't have any other valid reason for avoiding a relationship."

Jill swallowed, deeply admiring his honesty. And, oh, how her heart broke for him. He'd lost not only the woman he loved, but also his daughter's mother. While Doug had put Jill through emotional hell, she had no doubt that her experience had been nothing compared to what Brandon had gone through.

But she had to shove her sympathy aside and focus on the here and now. And here and now, she thought he was naive for discounting the fact that they both owned restaurants and that one would more than likely flourish at the expense of the other. That situation could definitely get nasty.

Those feelings aside, it was time for her to be as honest with him as he'd been with her, despite her unexpected emotional reaction to his visible pain, and even though the thought of sharing her deepest fears with him made her sweat. She'd work herself to a place where she could open up, though, if it meant getting Zoe and Kristy off the matchmaking bandwagon once and for all.

She looked right at him so he would know how determined she was for her restaurant to succeed, even if that success cost him. Being a successful, respected part of the Elm Corners business community was simply too important for her to back down for Brandon's sake.

"Well, I can't get around the whole business thing," she said, starting with the part that was easy to talk about. "I firmly believe that one of us is going to come out of this with their restaurant still standing, and I plan on it being me."

He nodded, his eyes alight with what looked like amusement.

Indignation flared hot and bright. His attitude fried her; Doug had always doubted her business abilities, thinking all she was good for was to stay home and take care of Zoe and the house. And the whole town thought of her only as Wacky's daughter, not someone who deserved respect.

"What, you don't think I'm capable of succeeding?" she asked, shoving her chin in the air.

"Let's just say I'm as determined as you are to be the lone fine-dining establishment in Elm Corners." He folded his hands on the table. "Go on."

Her indignation subsided. She had to admire the fact that he was just as determined as she was to succeed on the business front, even though he had a tougher row to hoe being the new guy in town.

"I wouldn't be so sure that you'll succeed," she said.

"Why is that?"

"I know from experience how hard it is to build a successful restaurant business that diverges from serving anything more sophisticated than burgers and fries." She gave him a steady look. "Especially in a traditional, set-in-its-ways place like Elm Corners."

"Really?" he asked, his voice full of doubt.

"Really," she said, giving an emphatic nod. "Heck, I know for a fact that people complain if the Elks Club doesn't serve chicken and potato salad every Tuesday night, as they've done for the last fifty years."

He laughed. "You're kidding."

She shook her head. "I'm dead serious. Worse, most of the town boycotted the Burger Barn last year because the owner started putting Swiss cheese on his burgers instead of the regular cheddar."

"I guess it's lucky that I'll be serving traditional fare like steak and potatoes, then."

He had a point, one that hadn't been lost on her, and had, in fact, bothered and worried her since she'd found out that a steak house was opening up right next door to The Grill. She served a continental selection of menu items at her restaurant, which, while fairly traditional, still flirted with a fusion style of cooking that many people in Elm Corners weren't interested in trying.

It was very likely that Brandon's more traditional eating establishment would do very well.

While her restaurant slowly went out of business.

So it was obvious he represented a direct threat to the further well-being of The Grill. But even if Brandon was the owner of the local circus she still wouldn't want any kind of personal relationship with him. He wanted to know why.

She twisted her hands into a knot in her lap. Doug had done a lot of damage, tearing her down, making her feel so vulnerable and worthless. Because of that she didn't like to open up about anything remotely personal. To her, that gave a man a kind of power over her she never wanted to relinquish again.

But she had to level with Brandon to find a way to get the girls off their parents' back.

She cleared her throat. "I'm divorced," she said baldly, her lingering bitterness toward Doug shining through. "For six years. Let's just say it wasn't pretty, and another woman was involved, a woman my ex-husband decided he wanted even though he was married to me and had a daughter."

"Ouch," Brandon said simply, sympathy obvious in his eyes.

She nodded tersely. "Yeah, it hurt, a lot, enough that I decided that love wasn't something I was ever going to let myself feel a second time. He dumped me and I never want to experience that again." Of course, she was leaving out a lot, things that were too deeply personal to share. How low her self-esteem had sunk after Doug left. How she'd felt like a total failure, so totally useless and unlovable.

So unworthy.

Brandon remained quiet for a few seconds. "Wow," he said, shaking his head, a crooked smile on his face. "Maybe we ought to start a club for all of the pitiful people out there who want to avoid love like we do."

Levity wasn't what she'd expected, but his amusing, totally accurate comment was just what she needed. She smiled back at him, thankful he'd accepted what she'd told him and hadn't probed any deeper.

"So now we know why a relationship won't ever work," she said, taking one last sip of coffee. "How in the world are we going to convince the girls to lay off?"

Before Brandon could respond, someone touched Jill on the arm. Jill turned and saw Leslie Shipley, Zoe's Girl Scout leader, standing next to her.

"Leslie, hi," Jill said, smiling. Zoe absolutely adored Leslie, who had made Girl Scouts both educational and interesting.

Leslie grinned back and gave a small wave. "Hey, Jill, Brandon. I'm so glad I found you two here," she said, her tone indicating she wondered exactly what kind of relationship the two of them had. "I just wanted to thank you both so much for volunteering to chaperone the field trip to Cannon Beach tomorrow."

Jill raised her eyebrows and looked at Brandon, her stomach plummeting. "I didn't know you were chaperoning, too," she said, her mouth barely moving, even though Leslie's news made sense, since Kristy was in the same Girl Scout troop Zoe was.

"Oh, Brandon signed up ages ago," Leslie interjected, laying a perfectly manicured hand on his shoulder.

Brandon nodded. "Kristy made me promise I'd go, since I'm not usually available for the field trips that take place during the week."

Jill digested that unexpected, troubling information, telling herself that just because Brandon was going on the field trip didn't mean they'd have to spend any time together.

"Zoe assured me you two would want to be a chaperone team," Leslie said, giving Jill a smile that looked pretty darn sly. The woman obviously thought Jill and Brandon were an item. "So I've taken the liberty of assigning you a group of five girls, including, of course, Zoe and Kristy. Since it looks like you guys are…acquainted, I'm sure you won't mind driving down to the beach together."

"I'm sorry," Jill immediately said, horrified. "But that's not going to work for me." Major understatement. The last thing she wanted to do was spend the whole day with Brandon in close quarters.

Leslie blinked. "Oh, dear. That's really going to put me in a bind. I can take the rest of the girls, but there isn't any extra space. Melanie Rutgers and her mom, the other chaperone, are going to meet us at the beach because they're down there already. So, you see, this is the only way it will work."

Jill opened her mouth to say she'd just drive down alone with Zoe, but remembered that her dad needed her car tomorrow, since a friend needed his truck to haul firewood. Mighty convenient, wasn't it? Curse him, anyway.

She clenched her jaw. While she really wanted to find a way out of this situation, she certainly didn't want to come across as uncooperative and selfish to Leslie when Leslie had done such a good job volunteering as the troop leader.

So she nodded feebly, feeling as if she were a puppet and Zoe and Kristy were pulling her strings. "Oh, I see. Then I guess we'll make the best of it." Although as far as Jill could see, "best" wasn't possible when she had to spend so much time with Brandon, restaurant owner extraordinaire.

Leslie nodded, looking relieved, then said goodbye.

Jill watched her go. "Darn Zoe," she said, shaking her head. "She's done it again."

"Yeah, it looks like she has," Brandon said, leaning back in his chair, a calculating gleam in his eyes. "But you know, I think we should just act like this is no big deal. Maybe if Zoe and Kristy see that forcing us together isn't going to work, they'll quit."

Jill threw him a doubtful look, her hands clenched into fists, hoping he was right. "You think?"

He sat forward, nodding. "Yup, I do. If we fight them, they'll just dig in their heels and work harder to manipulate us."

He had a good point. Maybe she and Brandon needed to take another tack. Maybe they needed to show the girls that their plan wouldn't work, no matter what they did.

Still, the thought of spending a whole day with him had giant butterflies dive-bombing in her stomach. He was a nice, considerate guy who seemed like a great father and was gorgeous to boot.

He was also a man she needed to dislike, a man who had the power to put her out of business.

A man she was extremely attracted to.

She only prayed that agreeing to go on this trip with him didn't blow up in her face.

Chapter Four

With five off-key, eight- and nine-year-old female voices filling his rig with the strains of "John Jacob Jingleheimer Schmidt," Brandon settled into the right lane of Highway 26 for the last fifteen minutes of the hour-and-a-half trip to Cannon Beach. He curved his mouth into a small grin. His daughter's joy, if nothing else, was music to his ears.

Bright blue sky peeked through the trees and the midmorning sun cast dappled shadows on the dashboard now and then. Looked as if the weather was going to be perfect for their day at the beach, a rarity on the Oregon coast in the unpredictable autumn months, when clouds, wind and drizzle beat out sunshine and clear skies much of the time.

One lone adult, on-key female voice wafted toward him. He glanced over at Jill sitting next to him in the passenger seat, softly singing along to the song. His heart rate kicked up a notch. Obviously she enjoyed the girls' singing as much as he did, even if the notes clashed rather than blended.

He let his gaze linger on her for a moment. He was still amazed at how pretty she looked dressed in jeans and a dark green sweatshirt, her hair pulled up into a casual ponytail, her blue eyes shining.

He was a sane driver and carried precious cargo, so he fought the urge to stare and shifted his gaze back to the road. He willed himself to ignore how damn attractive Jill was, determined to think of her only as his chaperone partner rather than as a woman he'd really, really like to kiss.

Sure, he'd been thrown for a loop when Leslie had announced he and Jill would be spending the day together as chaperones. A big one. While he thought Jill was taking the whole "conflict of interest" thing a bit too far, he wasn't an idiot. Being involved in any kind of personal way with someone he wanted to put out of business wasn't exactly brilliant.

But he was a rational person and a caring dad. So he'd agreed with Jill when she'd very grudgingly told him after Leslie left that they couldn't possibly ruin the field trip plans simply because they were business competitors.

He fully intended to set aside their adversarial business relationship for the duration of the field trip for the sake of a relaxing, stress-free, carefree day.

He glanced over at Jill. "You know this song?" he asked over the girls' "singing."

"Every former Girl Scout knows this song," she said, quirking her mouth into a grin. "I sang this back in the dark ages when I went to Girl Scout camp."

Before he could reply, he heard a loud giggle erupt from the back of his SUV. He looked in his rearview mirror and saw Kristy wedged in the far back between Zoe and Sarah. His daughter wore a bright smile on her face as she sang along to the silly song, and she looked happier and more content than he'd seen her in a long, long time. These girls, Zoe in particular, were obviously Kristy's friends, and she seemed to fit in just fine.

Feeling pretty content himself given his daughter's current state of happiness, he smiled broadly and shifted his gaze back to the road, negotiating a sweeping uphill curve. Thank goodness moving to Elm Corners was proving to be a good decision, at least for Kristy.

"Now, there's a big smile if I ever saw one," Jill said. "What's up?"

He shrugged, but his smile didn't fade. "I'm just happy to see Kristy making friends."

"Were you worried about that?" Jill shifted in her seat so she was looking directly at him. "She seems to be doing just fine."

"Sure I was worried. Moving and changing schools is hard, and since we arrived I've felt more than a little guilt about plopping Kristy down in a strange town." It remained to be seen whether his decision to ditch an established, lucrative career as an attorney for the uncertain world of owning a restaurant would end up being a business boon or a big, fat failure for himself.

"I know that feeling," she replied, her voice laced with sympathy. "Guilt and parenting seem to go hand in hand, don't they?"

"You've got that right. I felt guilty in L.A. for not spending much time with Kristy, and guilty for making her move so I could spend more time with her." He shook his head. "It seems like a no-win situation."

Jill shifted her eyes to the back of the rig. "Looks like it's a win-win situation now."

"I hope so," Brandon said. "Kristy's happiness is my number one priority."

Jill sat silent for a long moment, looking out the window, nibbling on a fingernail. "And I suppose making The Steak Place successful is your number two priority." Her voice had acquired a hard, cold edge that didn't bode well for his plan to forget about the competitive nature of their mutual careers for the day.

His hands gripping the steering wheel, he glanced at her, noting the stiffness in her lips and how tightly her hands were clenched together in her lap.

"This is a tense subject for you, isn't it?" he asked.

"Of course it is," she said, her lips barely moving. "Going out of business isn't exactly my idea of a relaxing subject."

"Then why did you bring it up?" He kept his voice low and quiet to soften the harshness of his question.

She gave a rough, under-the-breath laugh totally devoid of humor. "Boy, you don't pull any punches, do you?"

"Sometimes I do. But in this case, I'm only responding to the conversation you started." He glanced at her. "A conversation I'd rather just forget so we can enjoy the day."

"How am I supposed to do that? Three days ago I was ready to do the owner of The Steak Place bodily harm. It's not easy to just get rid of those feelings."

"Listen, I understand how you're feeling—"

"Really?" she interjected, her tone low and rife with sarcasm. "Do you really understand what it's like to work your butt off for two years to be successful, only to have someone else swoop in and threaten that success?"

Burning regret filled him, creating a hard knot in his chest. The day was going downhill, fast. "I hate that you think I'm nothing more than a big, mean restaurant ogre, out to do you wrong," he told her, struggling to keep his voice down now that the girls had stopped singing, though he doubted they'd hear him over their loud, giggle-strewn conversation.

"And I hate that I feel that way, but I do." She let out an audible breath. She whispered, "You're a threat to me, Brandon, a big one. And I'm having a hard time getting around that."

He gritted his teeth. Man, she was stubborn. "I can see that, and I'm sorry you feel so much animosity toward me. But the die's been cast and there's no going back for me. I came to Elm Corners with two very specific goals in mind." He raised two fingers to check them off. "To open a successful restaurant and spend more time with Kristy. No matter how much I wish I wasn't the person to jeopardize what you've worked so hard for, apparently I am. I don't see any way to change that."

"Neither do I, and that's the problem," she said. "Not exactly the best news for two people stuck together for the day, is it?"

"My thought exactly," he replied.

And just like that, his hopes for a carefree day disappeared.

Even though her brain was filled with upset and jumbled thoughts and her nerves were working overtime, Jill did her best to sit quietly as Brandon drove into the seaside town of Cannon Beach, Oregon. No sense in letting the girls know how agitated she was. She hoped none of them had noticed that she'd been chewing her fingernails to bits.

Not even the beautiful, blue-sky day and the quaintness so inherent in Cannon Beach's rustic wood storefronts, covered boardwalk and colorful flower boxes calmed her down.

Darn it all, Brandon was just too attractive for her

own good, all dark eyes and gorgeous smile, and it was eating away at her.

She had to get a grip if she was going to make it through this day with any sanity or fingernails left. Trouble was, she had no idea how to do that. He rattled her. Period.

Brandon pulled into a public parking lot in back of the stores on the main drag. Squealing, the girls jumped out the minute he stopped the car. Her shoulders tight, Jill climbed out without a word to Brandon, inhaling the fresh, salt-scented ocean air as if the clean breeze could blow all her troubles away.

She wished relaxing were that easy.

Zoe rounded the back of the car, looked at Jill and stopped in her tracks, her face pulled into a fierce frown. "Mom, what's wrong?" she asked. "You look kinda…mad or something."

Oh, boy, Jill thought. Was she lousy at hiding her feelings, or what? "Um…well…" She quickly pasted a smile on her face and relaxed her strained shoulders, determined not to ruin the girls' day because she was in a knot over Brandon. "I'm fine, honey, just feeling a little…carsick, that's all. But I'm better now."

"Oh, goody," Zoe said. "'Cause I want everybody to be in a good mood."

"I want that, too," Jill said, squeezing her daughter's shoulder. "Let's get our stuff out of the back."

Zoe ran around the back of the SUV and Jill stayed put for a moment, pressing a hand to the bridge of her nose, gathering her composure.

Zoe's concern had been a huge wake-up call; this day was important to the girls and Jill had no business ruining it. She was going to have to find a way to stuff away her conflicting emotions and act as if all was well in her world.

"You okay?" Brandon said.

Jill dropped her hand and looked at him, liking just a little too much the concern shining in his eyes. She made herself smile at him. "I'm fine…no, actually, I'm an idiot."

He drew in his chin. "Excuse me?"

"I said, I'm an idiot. I had no business letting my…personal feelings for you intrude on the girls' day."

Leaning in close, he said, "So you have *personal* feelings for me?" He wagged his eyebrows. "Really, Jill, isn't it a little soon for that?"

She stared at him for a second, noting the teasing light in his eyes, liking his attempt to pound some much-needed levity into her party-pooper frame of mind. "You're giving me a hard time, aren't you?"

He laughed, his straight white teeth flashing. "Of course I am. Nothing like a little good-natured ribbing to lighten the mood, wouldn't you say?"

She grinned back at him, this time actually feeling happy, and caught his gaze. "Yes, Mr. Clark, I would."

Instead of responding with words, he held her gaze with his whiskey-shaded eyes, and for a few incredible seconds it was impossible for Jill to look away, impossible to even breathe. Her grin faded from her lips and she fell into his eyes completely. Hot goose bumps shot up her spine, and excitement spiraled in her tummy like a kite dipping crazily in the wind.

"Dad!" Kristy said loudly from the back of the SUV, breaking the spell. "Let's go!"

Brandon looked away and Jill fell back a step, pressing a hand to her racing heart. She gulped in air, willing her suddenly blazing cheeks into cool submission.

"Um…well, do we have a truce?" she asked, surprised she could speak after getting snared in his one-of-a-kind eyes.

He turned back, nodding, the teasing light in his eyes gone, his jaw slightly tight. "I'm game if you are," he said. "Anything for the girls."

"Right. For the girls."

Then he spun around and moved to the back of the SUV, leaving Jill standing alone. She raised a shaking hand to her still-warm cheeks. What was she doing, letting her guard down, swapping hot, thrilling stares with Brandon? Yes, they needed to get along. Act like friends, even. But getting lost in his compelling gaze went way beyond that and crossed right into intensely personal, intensely dangerous territory.

For so many reasons, that was the last place she could let herself go.

An hour after they had arrived at Cannon Beach, Brandon helped Jill and Sarah spread two large blankets next to a huge log on the beach in preparation for eating a picnic lunch. The other girls, ten in total, played on the beach closer to the water, building sand castles and splashing a bit in the cold Pacific Ocean while Leslie, the troop leader, supervised.

Brandon put one of two large coolers on the edge of the blanket to hold it down in the wind. Jill did the same to the other blanket, joking around with Sarah, making the introverted girl smile and laugh.

Something in the vicinity of his heart twisted. He couldn't help but be hugely impressed by the way Jill had taken the shy Sarah under her wing for the day, spending extra time with the girl, encouraging her to help where needed, obviously making her feel special. It was so clear Jill was a genuinely nice, caring, sensitive woman.

He studied her, knocked almost speechless for what had to be the hundredth time by her fresh, natural beauty. She looked downright gorgeous with the beach breeze blowing her hair, her cheeks rosy, her mouth curved into a broad smile.

He pulled his gaze away, wishing he could manage to keep his eyes off her for a few minutes, wishing he wasn't so damn drawn to her when he needed to keep his distance.

Talk about a conflict of interest.

He shook his head and straightened the blanket, taming the urge to step close and lay a big kiss on her after he whispered in her ear how much he liked what she was doing for Sarah. Somehow he doubted Jill would appreciate that kind of move, and kissing her would be a major mistake. Once he did that…well, he suspected he'd have a hell of a time keeping her from digging under his skin.

"That should do it," Jill announced, her hands on her hips. "Sarah, honey, why don't you run down and tell the others it's time for lunch."

Sarah nodded and grinned, displaying a gap-toothed smile. "Okay, Mrs. Lindstrom." She took off across the sand, waving her arms, her long dark hair blowing in the breeze.

Following Jill's lead, Brandon knelt and opened the cooler to unload the sack lunches the girls had brought. "I like the way you've taken Sarah under your wing for the day," he said as he unpacked the cooler. "She likes you a lot." Hell, he knew how the kid felt.

Jill looked up from the cooler she was unloading. "She's brand-new to the troop, and doesn't know the other girls very well. I thought a little extra attention would ease her into spending the whole day with people she's just met." She sat back on her heels, a vague shadow growing in her bright blue gaze. "Besides, I was kind of shy when I was her age, so I know what it's like. My Girl Scout leader was extra nice to me and I've never forgotten it. I want to do the same for Sarah."

"You were shy?" Brandon asked, closing the cooler's lid. "Somehow I never pictured you that way. You seem so outgoing."

Jill started spreading the lunch bags out, keeping her gaze down. After a long silence she said, "When I was a kid, my dad's...uh, occupation made for a lot of teasing." She made a big show of flicking sand off the blanket. "So, well, I held back a lot, scared about how people were going to react."

He looked at her, sympathy bubbling to the surface. "Kids teased you a lot?"

"All the time."

His heart ached for what she'd gone through as a child. Before he could formulate an appropriate response, the girls showed up, a mass of wet, sandy feet, windblown hair and nonstop giggles.

Jill jumped up and passed around a damp towel to wipe off messy, salty hands, followed by a large squeeze bottle of antibacterial cleanser. He wouldn't have thought of that.

Everyone grabbed their lunches and sat around the outside of the blankets to chow down. By the time Brandon had his lunch in his hand, the only open space to sit was right next to Jill. Big surprise.

With a brow raised, he looked at Kristy. She met his suspicious gaze, smiled with no small amount of guilt, then nudged Zoe in the arm with her elbow. Zoe looked at him, blushed, then broke out into a fit of silly laughs.

Those two were incorrigible.

He let out a heavy breath, then moved to sit next to Jill. No use making a scene over a fifteen-minute lunchtime. Besides, he could think of a lot worse things than sitting beside a charming woman like Jill.

"They're at it again, aren't they?" Jill asked when he was settled.

He opened his lunch sack. "It seems they are. I hope you don't mind."

"Not at all," she said, one corner of her mouth lifting. "I assume we're still going with the 'let them see that getting us together isn't going to get us together' routine, right?"

"Right," he said, pulling out the ham sandwich he'd made himself this morning. "I'm confident they'll give up…eventually."

She rolled her eyes. "Like maybe in the next century?"

He laughed as he unwrapped his sandwich. "I like your ability to see the humorous side of all this."

"Trust me," she said, pointing at him with a slice of apple. "On the ride down, none of this seemed funny."

"I noticed. What changed?" he asked, curious how her mind worked, among other things.

She took a bite of her sandwich and chewed. "You really want to know?"

"Of course." He ripped the top off the bag of chips in his lunch sack.

"Well, I got out of the car feeling all doom and gloom and Zoe asked me what I was mad about."

"Go on," he said, liking the fact that it seemed she felt comfortable enough to be honest with him. Or at least he hoped so.

"When I realized my mood was so obvious, I decided I didn't want to ruin this trip for the girls simply because of the circumstances."

"Circumstances meaning me?" he asked, not about to bury his head in the sand about their adversarial relationship. Sandy's death had made him a die-hard realist.

She ducked her head, nodding. "Well…yes."

"Hey, you've been up-front from the get-go, so I'm perfectly aware that you'd rather not spend any time with me and I understand why. By the same token, I'm glad you've found a way to make this work." He didn't add that he was glad that his wish for a relaxing day was beginning to come true.

"So am I. I'm actually having a lot of fun, despite the company," she replied, throwing him a cute, teasing grin.

"Well, I don't know about that," he said, not above giving her a hard time. She was just so damn easy to tease. "Personally, I'm having a terrible time and I can't wait for the day to end."

"Yeah, right." She shook her head, grinning. "Anybody who wants blue sky, sunshine and sand and surf to end is crazy."

He crossed his eyes and yanked his lower lip down so it hung at an odd angle. "And how do you know I'm not crazy?" he asked her in a low, silly voice.

She giggled and touched his arm. "Now I'm not so sure you aren't."

Despite the heat and sparks her light touch caused, he managed to shrug and reply, "What can I say? I hide it well."

"Oh, I don't know about that," she said, smoothing a stray hair back from her face. "Any man who would willingly go on an all-day field trip with a carload of eight- and nine-year-old girls must have a screw loose somewhere."

He gave an exaggerated shake of his head, then stopped, as if listening. "Yeah, I can hear it rattling around in there."

She laughed again, a light, airy, feminine sound that moved across his heart like warm sunshine on a cold, dreary day, filling him with a kind of bright happiness and attraction he hadn't felt in a long, long time.

On one hand, that feeling pleased him and made him feel more alive than he'd felt in forever. How long had it been since he'd had any kind of meaningful conversation with a woman, much less actually enjoyed a moment so much?

On the other hand, that pleasure worried the hell out of him. It was dangerous. Threatening. Pretty risky to a man like him.

A man who had to protect his wounded heart no matter what.

Chapter Five

After lunch Jill, along with Brandon and the other chaperones, helped the girls clean up. When they were finished, everyone loaded up the cars to head to Haystack Rock a mile south of Cannon Beach for some tide-pooling.

As Brandon drove, Jill couldn't resist glancing over at him, remarkably quiet for a guy who had seemed so interested in talking at lunch. He looked really good, his short, dark hair mussed by the ocean breeze, his large hands handling the steering wheel with ease, his square jaw granite hard.

Butterflies took flight in her belly and she jerked her gaze back to the road ahead. As much as she tried to ignore how good it had felt to joke around with Brandon while they ate, his stunning smile weakening her knees, disregarding his appeal was proving to be irritatingly impossible. He was just so attractive. So much fun.

So darned fascinating.

She bit the inside of her lip and rolled her eyes. Why was she so enthralled by him, anyway? Sure, he was a good-looking, nice guy. But she met those kinds of men all the time in her business. Why was Brandon so different? Why did he draw her in so much, twisting her around until her heart was about to explode and she didn't know which way was up, much less how to kick him out of her brain?

She couldn't exactly put her finger on the answer, and that sad fact was driving her crazy. All she knew was that she didn't want to be so wrapped up in him. And she certainly didn't want to like his wicked sense of humor and how easily he could make her smile.

But there it all was in its disgusting glory. She was hugely captivated by a man she needed to shut out.

Great.

Their arrival at Haystack Rock precluded any chance to figure out how to keep a lid on her unfortunate but obvious attraction to one Mr. Brandon Clark.

She hastily decided that she just needed to get through the day, and then she'd be fine. He'd go his way, she'd go hers and that would be that. She'd ignore the depressing fact that Kristy and Zoe weren't likely to give up that easily.

Feeling marginally better, she climbed out of the car to herd the girls down the wooden stairs to the beach and Haystack Rock.

Thank heaven the weather was still cooperating. Other than a stiff breeze, practically a given on the Oregon coast, the blue sky and sunshine were holding.

The girls hit the beach and surged forward across the sand toward the giant haystack-shaped rock rising out of the water near the shore. One larger group went left with Leslie and the remainder went right with Brandon.

Jill's gaze caught on him running with three girls, holding Zoe's hand on one side and Sarah's on the other. They all scampered with open abandonment on the beach, their laughs twirling away on the sea-scented wind.

Why did he have to be so perfect?

That disturbing thought roiling around in her brain like a pot left too long to boil, she followed the group to the tide pools, mentally fastening on her armor.

"Mom!" Zoe called to her. "Come see the starfish!"

Jill walked over the hard-packed sand to the outermost tide pools where Zoe, Kristy, Sarah and Brandon crouched, their eyes fastened on the aquatic life before them.

"Aren't they cool?" Sarah asked, her eyes alight with excitement. "I like the orange ones."

Jill crouched down, too, and looked into the

shallow water left by the outgoing tide. "They're pretty, aren't they?"

"Beautiful," Brandon said, looking right at her, his eyes glowing with a dark, compelling light that stole her breath away.

Jill's jaw sagged and she stared at him, her heart pulsing like a drum in her chest. Had he actually just implied, out loud, that he thought she was beautiful? She popped up to a standing position, her legs unsteady.

He laughed, the dark light in his eyes turning bright and sparkling, then rose and came around to stand next to her. "The starfish, I mean," he mock-whispered. "I meant that the starfish were beautiful."

She nodded, her cheeks heating with a flush of un-expected pleasure, and fought the urge to fan her face with her hand. "I knew what you meant," she hastily assured him. "Really."

He gave her a wickedly crooked grin that set her heart racing into quadruple time all over again. "No doubt you did."

He ambled off with the girls to a different tide pool, and Jill followed, glad they were still in an area with a lot of sand. She doubted her unsteady, shaking knees would support her if she had to walk over the slippery rocks closer to the haystack.

She stopped and looked ahead, noting how the girls smiled adoringly at Brandon as he pointed into one of the tide pools. He said something and made a silly face and they all giggled.

Zoe and Kristy darted ahead of him, but he hung

back and waited for Sarah, then held out a hand to her as she gingerly negotiated the seaweed-covered rocks.

Jill's chest tightened, spreading softness and light throughout her, slowly eating away at the barrier around her heart. Not a good thing, but she seemed helpless to stop it.

She started walking again, her eyes on Brandon, her brain stuffed full of what a wonderful, considerate guy he was—and stepped right in the middle of a shin-deep, freezing-cold tide pool.

She let out a shriek, more out of irritation than anything else. How could she have been such an uncoordinated, idiotic clod? Clearly, Brandon unsettled her in a big, big way.

Brandon came running. "Jill! What's wrong?"

She pulled her dripping foot out of the pool and gave him a sheepish grin, her cheeks warming. "I…uh, was distracted," she said, leaving out that she'd been distracted by *him*. No way was she going to let him know that he affected her ability to walk around large pools of water. "I kind of…fell in."

He put his hands on her shoulders and looked at her, his expression solemn, his eyes alight with alarm. "You're not hurt, are you?"

She shook her head, liking his concern, intensely aware of his big warm hands on her, his warmth seeping clear down to her skin, even through her thick sweatshirt and cotton top. "No, just embarrassed. Not exactly a graceful move." Or a comfortable one. A waterlogged, cold tennis shoe, sock and pant leg weren't exactly her idea of pleasant, especially with the wind.

"No need to be embarrassed," he said with an indulgent, calming smile she could get used to—fast. "Did you bring any dry clothes?"

She shook her head. "No, I didn't exactly plan on getting wet." Or on making a total fool of herself. Honestly, what in the name of heaven was wrong with her?

"I have an extra pair of sweatpants in the car, along with some dry socks. Why don't we go back up to the car and you can change?"

She backed up a step, shaking her head. "Oh, no, that's all right," she said, waving a negligent hand in the air. The thought of actually wearing Brandon's clothes seemed way too personal, given how long it had been since she'd shared any kind of intimacy with a man. "With this breeze, I'll be dry in no time."

"You'll also freeze in no time."

"Nah, I'll be fine, really." Fine, but cold. And wet. And sloshy. Ugh.

He pressed his lips into a firm line and gave her a stern look. "Jill, I insist you change into my clothes. I'm sure you don't want me worrying about you for the rest of the day, do you?"

"Actually, I don't." The thought of him hovering over her all day, his warm brown eyes alight with concern, made her sweat.

"Then be smart and do what I say."

She rolled her eyes. "Are you always this...bossy?"

"Always," he assured her. "Now, let's go get you out of those clothes." He gestured in the direction of his SUV.

His caring so much about her comfort made her feel all warm and toasty inside, and that scared the devil out of her. In an attempt to make light of some heavy emotions, she gave in to her wicked side and said, "So you'll be helping me?" She threw him an impish grin so he'd know she was teasing.

He stilled, then turned and regarded her levelly, his chestnut eyes drilling into her like a hot, tingly laser. "Only if you want me to."

Her cheeks fired up again and she instantly regretted her suggestive comment, which she now realized walked the fine line between good-natured teasing and outright flirting. Maybe even crossed it.

Her breath left her in a rush. Good heavens, she was flirting with him!

Struggling to breathe, she locked on his gaze, unable to look away, swaying slightly toward him. Deep down where she didn't look very often, the thought of him helping her out of her clothes lit a long-dormant fire inside her, scorching her from the inside out. As if by magic, thoughts of her and Brandon, alone, losing themselves in each other burned through her mind—

Out of sheer instinct she jerked her gaze from his and managed to say, "I was just kidding" in an amazingly normal voice, even though her emotions were spinning wildly out of control again.

Wonderful. Weak knees and a mushy, unguarded heart. Flirting. Stupid thoughts about getting personal with Brandon. Out-of-control emotions she didn't ever want to deal with again.

A new kind of dread worked its way through her, setting her nerves on a hard edge.

Brandon was a huge temptation, no doubt about it. She prayed she had the power to resist him.

An hour after Jill had stepped into the tide pool and soaked her leg, Brandon lowered himself to the sand to sit next to her as she watched the girls build a giant sand castle, with Leslie a few yards away.

The breeze had calmed and the sun was amazingly warm on his face—not that he needed warming since Jill had joked about him helping her out of her clothes. Hell, no. He'd been smoldering since then.

He'd known she was teasing him, of course, but her suggestive comment had still sent hot excitement shooting through him like a firecracker on the Fourth of July. An excitement that was still burning through him now.

Okay. So he was in major lust with her. He could handle that, right? It was just a physical thing, nothing more than basic biology at work, and he'd always prided himself on his ability to control himself physically. A requirement for a man who wasn't looking to take another ride on the heartbreak express.

Besides, if Jill had her way, they would never lay eyes on each other again after today. Out of sight, out of mind as the saying went. Sounded good to him. Sort of…

"Thanks again for the pants," Jill said. "Big is better than wet."

He turned toward her and smiled. "Glad I had them on hand. Sorry I didn't have shoes you could wear."

She lifted one slender shoulder. "That's okay. Luckily it's warm enough now to go barefoot."

He looked down at her toes curled in the sand, noticing some kind of pink-and-blue swirling pattern painted on her toenails. "What's up with your toenail polish?"

She lifted her feet and wiggled her toes. "Zoe's attempt at painting flowers."

He craned his neck to get a better view. "Flowers, huh?"

She laughed. "I know. Looks more like blobs than flowers. But she insisted. Who was I to argue?"

Brandon had to admire her indulgent nature. "Quite frankly, I don't get the whole nail-polish fascination girls have." He propped his elbows on his raised knees. "Every time we go to Target, Kristy has to buy at least three new bottles."

"I hear you. I counted last week. Zoe has fifteen colors, including sparkles," Jill said. "Give me plain old pink any day."

"Yeah, well, even plain old pink stains the carpet. We found that out the hard way."

Jill put a hand over her mouth to cover her grin. "I'm sorry."

He shrugged. "Live and learn. Now if I can just figure out how to French braid her hair, I'll be set." Although deep down he was struggling to relate to his daughter on many different levels.

"Hey, even I'm no good at that," she replied, waving a hand in the air. "So don't feel bad."

He appreciated her attempt to make him feel better. "That's odd, because Kristy always raves about how much she likes Zoe's French-braided hair."

"My dad does it."

He hoisted his eyebrows. So much for a guy having a hard time with girlie stuff. "Really?"

"Really. I wanted French braids in the worst way when I was about Zoe and Kristy's age, and I begged him for weeks. Finally, one day he magically produced an instruction book and studied and practiced on me until he got it down." She smiled crookedly. "Now he's a bona fide expert. You should see him go."

"I'll have to bow down in admiration and respect the next time I see him," Brandon said. "I tried once, and my hands cramped up and Kristy's hair looked like something had exploded in it."

Jill rubbed her chin. "Come to think of it, years ago I think he was even working on a contraption to help hold the hair, or something like that."

"Whatever happened to it?"

She looked out at the sun-speckled ocean, her lips tightening. "The same thing that happens to all of his inventions." She let out a huffy breath. "Nothing."

"Nothing?" he asked, noting the irritated edge to her voice.

She nodded. "Yup, nothing. It didn't work, and he lost interest and moved on. The thing—I remember it was made of wire—is probably lying around his workshop somewhere, gathering dust."

He sensed the tension in her words, noticed how stiff her shoulders had become. There was an unmistakable contrast between how she'd spoken about her dad when she was talking about him learning to braid her hair and how she was speaking about him now, and that intrigued him.

He chewed on the inside of his cheek. Should he go on? Was this a touchy subject for her?

His curiosity about what made her tick won out. "Has your dad always been an inventor?"

She looked away and drew doodles in the sand with her fingers. "For as long as I can remember," she said, bitterness creeping into her tone. "He's never done anything else."

He recalled what she'd told him about how the other kids had given her a hard time about her dad exploding things when she was growing up. Okay, so talking about her dad's career *was* a sensitive subject for her.

He sat silently for a moment, sympathy burning in his chest, watching a seagull soaring over the ocean. How should he proceed with their conversation? He certainly wasn't an expert when it came to relationships, but he was smart enough to sense when someone was angry about something, and he was really interested—too interested, probably—in what had made her the incredible woman she was today.

Leaning forward, he looked at her averted face. "Do you want to talk about it?" he asked, even though he was pretty sure she'd clam up and shut down his question-and-answer session. It was no secret she didn't view him as anything more than a nasty problem she'd been forced to deal with rather than as a friend.

"About what?" she asked, still looking at the sand, the delicate line of her jaw noticeably rigid.

"Why you resent your dad's occupation so much," he replied, though he really didn't expect an answer.

"I don't resent that he's an inventor," she said, her thinned lips and stiff posture belying her words. She lifted her head and huffed. She looked right at Brandon, one brow arched. "Why would I?"

"Oh, come on. Your body language screams resentment. But why…" He shook his head. "Well, I have no idea."

She didn't answer him for a long time. Finally she said in a very small voice, "Why couldn't he be an accountant or a banker or a grocery store clerk?"

"So it was hard being his daughter?" he asked, surprised yet pleased that she was opening up to him.

She hugged her knees with her slender arms. "You could say that."

"How was it hard?"

She sighed and rested her chin on her knees. "Do you have any idea what it's like to grow up as the child of Wacky Winters, the town joke and resident mad scientist?"

"Why don't you tell me."

"It was…embarrassing." She turned her head and looked at him, her blue, blue eyes reflecting a heavy, enduring sadness that twisted his heart into a knot. "He was different from my friends' dads, and was always blowing up his lab, walking around with his hair sticking up and his clothes covered in whatever exploded on him that day." She raised her head from her knees and looked away, swallowing. "Nobody respected him, Brandon, and I've lived in that shadow for a long time."

He stared at her, wanting to take her into his arms, wipe away her sadness and make everything right in her world. But he doubted she'd appreciate his comfort, and he knew better than anyone that he couldn't wave a magic wand and fix her pain or heal her emotional wounds.

"I'm sorry," he said, meaning it. "But, you know, I met your dad a while ago, and I respected him from the start, despite his…unique appearance. Maybe he's earned more respect than you think."

She looked out at the ocean for a few long moments. "You're sweet to say that—"

"I'm not saying it to be sweet," he said. "It's the truth."

"Well, either way, I appreciate the thought." She looked at him, her eyes now reflecting steel-edged determination. "Maybe things will be different now that I've been given a chance to prove myself as someone other than Wacky's daughter."

Vague dread tiptoed up his spine. "And how will you do that?" he asked, even though he was pretty sure he already knew what she was going to say.

And that he was going to feel like a heartless heel when that fact was confirmed.

"As a successful restaurant owner, of course," she said, never looking away from him.

His chest nearly collapsed, even though he'd been right on the money about what she was going to say. She wanted her restaurant to be a success to gain the respect of the people of Elm Corners, the respect she felt she'd been denied her whole life because of her father.

Brandon swallowed the burning lump of regret in his throat and studied the sand at his feet, unable to look her in the eye, gaining new understanding about why she resented him so much.

Because if things went as planned, he'd be the man to snatch her success and respect right out from under her by putting her out of business. Or at the very least by taking some or most of her customers away.

Right on schedule, just as he'd feared, he felt like that heartless heel five times over.

It was the crummiest feeling he'd had in a very long time.

Jill looked at Brandon when he didn't say anything. She noted the grim line of his lips, the sudden rigidity in his shoulders and how he was suddenly very, very interested in looking at anything but her.

She peeled her gaze from him and shifted uneasily on the sand, watching the girls and Leslie dig a deep moat around their newly constructed sand castle. On a deep sigh Jill moved her feet until she was sitting cross-legged, feeling chilled despite the warmth of the sunny day.

What had she been thinking, opening up to him when he was the one person who could smash her dreams into pieces? She shouldn't have let the conversation get so personal, much less let him in on her own private demons.

She shouldn't have given him so much power.

But at the time, it had just seemed so...well, right. So necessary. Especially since he'd seemed genuinely interested and she hadn't unloaded on anyone in a really long time.

Well, she'd had a brain burp and had chosen the wrong guy to talk to. Darn him, anyway, for acting like the perfect person to dump on when she shouldn't be dumping on anyone.

She looked at him again, his stiff posture still noticeable. A startling thought occurred to her. "Brandon, I didn't let you in on my personal problems to make you feel sorry for me, you know."

He turned and looked at her. "How did you know that's what I was thinking?"

She lifted one shoulder, slightly disappointed that she'd read him right. "Woman's intuition."

Play the Lucky Hearts Game

and get...

2 FREE BOOKS

and a **FREE MYSTERY GIFT...**

yes! **YOURS to KEEP!**

I have scratched off the silver card. Please send me my *2 FREE BOOKS* and *FREE mystery GIFT.* I understand that I am under no obligation to purchase any books as explained on the back of this card.

Scratch Here!

then look below to see what your cards get you... 2 Free Books & a Free Mystery Gift!

310 SDL EFWW   **210 SDL EFVM**

FIRST NAME

LAST NAME

ADDRESS

APT.#

CITY

STATE/PROV.

ZIP/POSTAL CODE

(SL-R-06/06)

Twenty-one gets you
2 FREE BOOKS
and a **FREE MYSTERY GIFT!**

Twenty gets you
2 FREE BOOKS!

Nineteen gets you
1 FREE BOOK!

TRY AGAIN!

Offer limited to one per household and not valid to current Silhouette Romance® subscribers. All orders subject to approval. Please allow 4-6 weeks for delivery.

The Silhouette Reader Service™ — Here's how it works:

Accepting your 2 free books and mystery gift places you under no obligation to buy anything. You may keep the books and gift and return the shipping statement marked "cancel." If you do not cancel, about a month later we'll send you 4 additional books and bill you just $3.57 each in the U.S., or $4.05 each in Canada, plus 25¢ shipping & handling per book and applicable taxes if any.* That's the complete price and — compared to cover prices of $4.25 each in the U.S., and $4.99 each in Canada — it's quite a bargain! You may cancel at any time, but if you choose to continue, every month we'll send you 4 more books which you may either purchase at the discount price or return to us and cancel your subscription.

*Terms and prices subject to change without notice. Sales tax applicable in N.Y. Canadian residents will be charged applicable provincial taxes and GST. Credit or debit balances in a customer's account(s) may be offset by any other outstanding balance owed by or to the customer.

BUSINESS REPLY MAIL
FIRST-CLASS MAIL   PERMIT NO. 717-003   BUFFALO, NY

POSTAGE WILL BE PAID BY ADDRESSEE

SILHOUETTE READER SERVICE
3010 WALDEN AVE
PO BOX 1867
BUFFALO NY 14240-9952

NO POSTAGE
NECESSARY
IF MAILED
IN THE
UNITED STATES

If offer card is missing write to: The Silhouette Reader Service, 3010 Walden Ave., P.O. Box 1867, Buffalo, NY 14240-1867

"Ah, that." Regret began to burn in his eyes. "I'm sorry to admit I was wishing you hadn't told me all of that because it makes it harder for me to put you out of business."

She held up a hand, palm out, determined to stay rational. "Don't apologize, Brandon. Even though I hate the reason you're bothered by what I told you, you're entitled to feel that way." She forced herself to smile. "And at least I know now that you have a conscience, right?"

"Did you doubt I did?"

She inclined her head, thinking. "I hadn't really thought about it one way or another," she said truthfully.

"And here I thought you saw me as one great big bogeyman." He tugged his mouth into a wry smile.

"Well, actually, I kind of did see you that way. I guess I just hadn't put all of that into concrete, distinct terms like whether you had a conscience or not."

He stretched his legs out in front of him and leaned back on his hands. "So now do you understand that I'm just a regular guy trying to make a living and not some shark out to ruin your life?"

"I get that," she said honestly. "Any guy who is as devoted to his daughter as you obviously are can't be a really bad person."

He inclined his head, presumably to acknowledge her compliment. "And do you understand that I have very important reasons for wanting to make my business a success, too, and that I want to be successful for my own reasons rather than to simply put you out of business?"

"Does it really matter what I think?" she asked solemnly, stalling, not sure she really wanted to know precisely why success was so important to him. The more she knew about him, the more human he became.

And the more human he became, the more likely it was that she might let herself care about him.

Darn him for putting out the bait, anyway.

He remained silent for a moment. "Even though it's crazy, your opinion matters to me."

Her stomach lurched and a warm, wonderful feeling settled in her chest, whittling down her resistance to getting to know the real Brandon.

The fact that he cared what she thought shouldn't matter one bit. But his respect did matter. A lot. More than it should. "Well, then, yes, I understand all of that. All of it except what your reasons are," she said, like a fool taking the bait he'd thrown out, diving headfirst into a dangerous place she'd sworn she'd avoid.

He pierced her with those dark, seductive eyes of his. "You really want to know?"

A hot chill skittered through her. Unfortunately, she did want to know, even though knowing anything remotely personal about him would undoubtedly take her nearer to actually caring about him. "Yes, I do."

"Fair enough." He lay back on the sand, cradling his head in his hands. "First off, I grew up in the restaurant business in L.A. and have always wanted to own a restaurant."

She looked down the beach and saw the girls happily digging a huge hole in the sand, Leslie nearby, supervising. Confident all was well with them, she lay down on her side next to him, resting her head on her upper arm, careful to maintain a good distance from Brandon. "So why did you become a lawyer?"

"My dad steered me away from the restaurant business. Thought it was too unstable, too demanding. And don't get me wrong, I loved my job in L.A. But after Sandy died and I became a single dad, working fifteen-hour days was impossible. I never saw Kristy, and suddenly she was closer to the nanny than she was to me."

Jill swallowed, aching at the residual pain so evident in his voice.

"That really got me," he said, continuing. "So I decided to invest my life savings in opening The Steak Place, starting a restaurant like I'd always dreamed of doing. I chose Elm Corners because I wanted to raise Kristy in a small, traditional town and also because I didn't want to own a trendy place in L.A. that would demand just as many hours as my job as an attorney had. This way, Kristy can come to the restaurant after school and hang out, and I can work fewer hours."

She ignored how knowing that he'd invested his life savings in his restaurant venture made her feel slightly ill—his bid for success had suddenly taken on a personal significance she'd hoped to avoid— and skewered him with a pointed look. "And because you knew that the competition was limited."

"Well, yes, and because of that, too. But mainly I wanted to settle in a family kind of place where Kristy would thrive." He smiled, his face lighting up, love for his daughter very, very evident in his soft brown eyes. "And she is. She's made a few good friends, Zoe in particular, and she's loving school and her Girl Scout troop."

Jill's insides turned to pure mush. Even though she didn't want to, she liked and respected him. A lot. He was putting his daughter first, and that meant he was a stellar dad in her world, where her ex-husband could barely manage to see his own daughter once a month.

She suddenly saw Brandon in a whole new light. A very, very good light.

She bit her lip as more guilt roiled through her. "Maybe you shouldn't have told me all that."

"Why?"

She lifted one shoulder. "Now that I know why it's so important you succeed, I feel guilty."

He looked at her, frowning. "Guilty?"

"Yes, guilty. It's entirely possible my success will come at your expense." That idea lurched around her like a greasy meal; he was a good man with very valid, altruistic reasons for wanting to succeed. "I'm not sure I'm willing to be the person to ruin that for you."

He sat up and leaned close to whisper in her ear,

his warm breath raising hot chills. "I hate to be the one to point this out, but I may be the one who succeeds at your expense."

"And that makes me feel bad, too," she said, liking his nearness just a little too much even as the truth in his words cut through her as cleanly as a chef's knife. "Not exactly a win-win situation, is it?"

"I guess not," he said, moving away and rolling to his feet. "And unfortunately, I'm in the same boat, aren't I?"

She looked right at him, her expression solemn, reflecting how the truth was a real bummer—for both of them. "I guess you are."

"I'm going to check on the girls, all right?" he said, heading toward them as they returned to work on the giant sand castle they'd built.

She nodded absently, glad for some space and some time to consider her conflicting emotions.

She stood and began to pace. All she could think about was that liking and respecting and admiring Brandon as much as she did was bad. It would be so much easier to keep him out of her thoughts if she could simply hate him, dismiss him, forget him and move on.

A bad feeling settled in the pit of her stomach. Obviously forgetting Brandon Clark wasn't going to be easy.

He was a good man. And that was a terrible thing for a woman who could never, ever allow herself to love him.

Chapter Six

Two days after the beach trip Brandon drove home from the restaurant, weary after a long day of meetings and interviews. He was close to hiring a manager and had narrowed his choices for a head chef down to three. Work was going well.

Too bad his personal life wasn't. Damn, it would be nice if the beautiful day had the power to cheer him up.

But bright sun and gorgeous skies couldn't take his mind off how much he'd been thinking about Jill. So much, in fact, that he'd lain awake every night since they'd talked on the beach, her heartfelt confessions swirling in his mind like bad reruns on late-night TV.

As he'd lain there in his solitary bed, his thoughts had veered wildly between how he wanted to soothe Jill's pain and make everything right in her world and how, if he made The Steak Place a success, he'd only be adding to her pain. Funny how that idea had made his chest burn and his stomach twist.

To add to his problems, he hadn't been sleeping well. Every night after he'd finally fallen into a deep sleep near dawn, he'd dreamed of a soft, flower-scented Jill lying next to him in bed, her legs entwined around him, her heart beating in time with his.

Each morning he'd awakened happy, believing a warm, sleepy Jill was in bed next to him. Man, had he been disappointed when he'd discovered that she was just a damn dream.

He pounded the steering wheel. He shouldn't be thinking about her, much less fantasizing about her. Jill had made her wishes clear—she was determined to stay away from any kind of relationship for very good reasons—and every protective instinct inside him warned him to walk away. Walk away, walk away.

He pulled into the driveway and saw Kristy playing in the front yard with Shelby, the teenage neighbor girl who watched Kristy after school when he had meetings away from the restaurant he couldn't take Kristy to.

Though he'd been putting off the chore, he needed to talk to Kristy as he'd promised Jill he would. Frankly, he'd been surprised that he and Jill hadn't already been hit with another scheme to get them together. Kristy and Zoe were remarkably determined and resourceful for two young girls who couldn't even stay home alone yet.

Luckily they hadn't pulled another matchmaking stunt. Although the thought of being thrown together with the wonderful, beautiful, appealing Jill sounded pretty good....

Kristy greeted him with a hug and a kiss. After he paid Shelby and she went home, he herded his daughter inside and set out hamburger to make spaghetti—Kristy's favorite. He then called her into the kitchen so he could talk to her while he cooked.

"So, Kris, how was your day?" he asked, easing into the conversation. "Anything exciting happen at school?"

She hoisted herself onto a bar stool next to the eating bar. "Jimmy Pruitt fell down on the playground and had to get stitches."

"Really? That's too bad." Brandon pulled out the frying pan for the spaghetti sauce. "Did you finish that book you've been so interested in? The one about wizards?"

She nodded. "Yup, in class today."

"Good job, honey." He was pleased that Kristy was finally getting into reading, a subject that had never held much appeal for her in the past. He thanked the influence of her teacher, who apparently made reading fun. He was happy to admit that their move to Elm Corners had been a good choice for Kristy in many ways. "Listen, I need to talk to you about...what you and Zoe have been doing."

Her face went totally blank and she was suddenly extremely interested in studying the pattern on the counter. "Wh-what do you mean?"

He pulled out a knife and opened the package of hamburger, then turned on the heat beneath the frying pan. "Kris, I'm sure it's kind of a secret, but I know that you and Zoe have been fixing it so me and Mrs. Lindstrom are…thrown together."

Kristy remained silent, simply staring at him, her brown eyes wide and still.

He forged ahead. "Anyway, Mrs. Lindstrom and I don't want to…date."

"Why not?" Kristy blurted, her expression instantly changing from blank to a tight-lipped pout. "She's really nice."

"Yes, she is." She was too nice. Too perfect. Too appealing. "But both of us have reasons for not wanting to fall in love again, and you and Zoe need to respect those reasons and back off."

"So you're saying you're never going to fall in love again?" Kristy asked in a very small, very sad voice that ripped his insides to shreds.

He wished with everything in him that things were different and he could make her dreams for a mom come true. But that was impossible. He dumped the hamburger into the pan and began to break it up with a wooden spoon. He opened his mouth to say, "Yes, never," but clamped it shut again and absently stirred the hamburger, his belly caving in little by little. As idealistic as Kristy was, she'd posed an excellent question.

A question he'd thought he knew the answer to. Now he wasn't so sure.

He reduced the heat under the burger and grabbed a jar of spaghetti sauce, his brain humming. Was he really willing to spend the rest of his life cut off from love, by choice, never again knowing the joy of loving a woman?

He shook his head. What had once been a no-brainer—no love, no pain, period—suddenly seemed hard to wrap his thoughts around. He had Jill and her charm, her bright smile and compassionate, kind personality to thank for that.

"Dad, did you hear me?" Kristy asked, jerking him from his chaotic thoughts.

"Maybe never," he said to Kristy as a compromise. "The future is hard to predict, honey, so that's the best I can do. But I do know that you and Zoe need to back off with the matchmaking scheme. As sweet as it is, I don't need you playing Cupid for me, okay?"

After a long pause, she said, "I guess" in a flat voice that conveyed quite well what she thought of what he'd said. He had a bad feeling this whole invention plan of theirs wasn't over.

She then hopped down from the bar stool, her small shoulders slumped in defeat. "I'm going to read my book until dinner."

She left Brandon alone in the kitchen, his gut in a wad. He hated disappointing her, but it couldn't be helped. For everyone's well-being she and Zoe had to lay off. Now.

He shifted his attention to what Kristy had said about him never loving again, and his thoughts began sizzling and popping like the hamburger on the stove.

Was never loving a woman again a sacrifice he was willing to make to protect himself from loss? Was he really prepared to be alone *forever?*

He had no idea, and that was bad. What he did know was that Jill had broken through his self-protective barrier and taken up permanent residence in his mind.

Did he have the strength to kick her out of his brain—and his life—forever?

As much as he hated to admit it, he was beginning, little by little, to doubt that he did.

Jill wiped some flour from her hands and stepped out from The Wildflower Grill's kitchen into the dining room. Though the lunch crowd had thinned out, the place had been packed earlier. She smiled.

For weeks, she'd been working on fine-tuning her lunch menu, hoping to draw customers in with lighter yet tasty lunch fare, and it looked as if her hard work was paying off. The Grill was doing very well. At least today.

But what about when The Steak Place opened up two doors down? Then her success and bid for respect would be in jeopardy. Because of one man.

Her smile faded.

Brandon.

Her jaw clenched, she headed for her small office next to the kitchen. Why couldn't she get him out of her mind? Why couldn't she just hate him, go for the jugular and feel okay about being the one to ruin his dreams of success in Elm Corners?

Why did she have to keep remembering how patient he'd been with the girls, how they'd all loved his jokes on the beach trip and how every time he looked at her, she almost melted? How she'd been fantasizing for the three days since they'd returned from the beach about what it would be like to kiss him all night long? How he was just being a good dad, trying to do what was best for his daughter, an extremely admirable goal?

Her conflicting thoughts were driving her crazy, twisting and turning in her head until she wanted to wave her fists in the air and scream.

On the way to her office she passed Melanie, her manager, who was coming out of the kitchen. As usual, Mel had her long dark hair tied back in a low ponytail.

Melanie smiled, her dark-brown eyes flashing, and then did a double take. "Hey, who died?"

Jill scrunched her eyebrows together. "Huh?"

"You look like somebody died." Melanie laid a hand on Jill's forehead for a moment. "You sick or something?"

Jill shook her head. "I'm just a little…upset, that's all."

"Ah, the vegetable delivery," Melanie said, nodding. "Yeah, the broccoli looked pretty bad, didn't it?"

Jill sighed. "I wish my only problem was rotten

vegetables." She started moving again, heading for her office.

Melanie followed. "So what *is* the problem?"

Jill bit her lip. Mel had been with her since Jill had decided to open a restaurant, through all her ups and downs. Maybe Jill would feel better if she talked to Mel about her contradictory, exasperating feelings for Brandon. She doubted it was possible to feel worse.

"Uh…well, there's this guy I met—"

"You're dating a guy? Who is he? Does he have a friend or a brother?"

Jill quelled her irritation as she entered her tiny office, complete with antique desk, framed motivational posters on the walls and numerous potted plants. Melanie was perpetually single, much to her irritation, and wanted to be attached in the worst way. The petite brunette was constantly lamenting the lack of eligible men in Elm Corners, a fact that Jill hadn't ever even noticed.

"Wait a minute," she said to Melanie, holding her hands up in the air. "I said I met a guy, not that I was dating him."

Melanie's face fell. "Oh. So what's the problem?"

"We're not dating, but I keep thinking about him."

"And this would be a bad thing?" Melanie asked, crossing her arms over her chest, giving Jill a look, the one that said she thought Jill was off her rocker for believing that thinking about a guy was a negative thing.

"Of course it's a bad thing." Jill sat behind her desk. "You know how much Doug hurt me when he left and that I'm not interested in reliving that kind of pain."

"Yeah, yeah, the whole avoid-love-to-protect-yourself routine. I get it—and think it's stupid."

Jill shot her a hard glare. "Gee, thanks for the support, Mel."

"I'm sorry about the way that came out," Mel said, her eyes alight with contrition. "But, hey, Jill, I just feel it's my duty to be truthful. You're a wonderful, loving woman who shouldn't be alone for the rest of your life, that's all."

A shaft of sadness pierced Jill. Suddenly that solitary life now loomed before her like a black hole. "I appreciate your thoughts, but I haven't told you everything."

"Spill it," Melanie said, propping a hip on the edge of Jill's desk.

"He's Brandon Clark, owner of The Steak Place."

For a second Melanie's face went blank. Then she lifted her chin and raised her eyebrows. "Ah. The competition."

"Exactly," Jill said, pointing a rigid finger at Melanie. "He could ruin me, and all I can think about is how great a dad he is and how nice he is and how every time he looks at me I get tingles shooting up my spine."

"So you like the guy. Nothing wrong with that, right?"

"Did you hear the word *ruin,* Mel?"

"Oh, I heard it, don't worry. But we're talking about a good-looking, eligible man and around here, those kind are few and far between. I say go for it."

"And what if he puts me out of business, or vice versa? There'll be bad feelings all over the place. One of us is bound to get hurt."

Mel leaned down and skewered her with a hard yet compassionate gaze. "So if it's you, you pick yourself up and move on. Besides, maybe it'll work out and you'll live happily ever after." She grinned. "It does happen once in a while, you know."

"Yeah, well, I don't have any personal experience with happily-ever-after, so please excuse me if I don't hop on the love train anytime soon. Brandon may be the most charming, attractive man I've ever met, but I still have to keep my distance."

Before Mel could respond, Kate, the afternoon hostess, popped her head into the office. "Someone out front to see you, Jill."

"Who is it?"

"Brandon Clark."

Jill's stomach knotted and her heart rate shot up. "Th-thank you, Kate."

"I guess this Brandon guy doesn't want to keep *his* distance, does he?" Mel said, her mouth curved into a knowing smile. "Wouldn't it be cool if you had an admirer?"

Jill rolled her eyes even as, surprisingly, the thought of Brandon being her admirer didn't sound all that bad.

Obviously she was losing her mind. "He's probably just here to talk about Zoe and his daughter, Kristy."

"He could call you on the phone to do that," Mel shot back. "He's here in person." She waggled her eyebrows. "Ten dollars says he's hot for you."

Jill stood and waved Mel off. "Oh, stop, would you?" she said. "I'm sure it's nothing like that."

After she removed her dark green apron and smoothed her hair—Mel snickered—Jill left Mel in her office and headed down the hall to the front desk. Butterflies took crazy flight in her tummy and anticipation roared to brilliant life deep down inside her.

She had to admit that the thought of seeing Brandon again lifted her spirits and brought light into her shadowed, lonely heart.

For the life of her, she couldn't make herself believe that could be bad.

Chapter Seven

Brandon stood in the entryway to The Wildflower Grill, waiting to see Jill. He forced himself not to fidget; in keeping with his determination to kick Jill out of his thoughts, this wasn't a social call.

He was here for two very specific reasons. To check out the competition and talk to Jill about his suspicions regarding Kristy and Zoe. That was it.

Even so, his nerves ratcheted up at the thought of seeing Jill again. Given the competitive nature of their relationship, it was entirely possible she might tell him off and kick him out onto the street.

In the interest of actually checking out The Grill, he looked around, admiring the decor of her restaurant. The walls were painted a rich shade of sage-green that complemented the numerous green potted plants she'd placed throughout the smallish space. Softly lit wood-framed paintings of different plants and flowers hung on every wall. Soft, piped-in piano music played in the background.

In deference to the name of the restaurant, he supposed, she'd placed large bouquets of vibrant wildflowers on every available surface, creating a colorful yet tranquil atmosphere. Wood ceiling fans that matched the tables spun lazily above the diners and a soothing waterfall surrounded by greenery in the corner added to the unmistakably relaxing ambience.

He rocked back on his heels, admiration flaring to life. He had to give her a ton of credit. She'd taken what looked to have been a fairly small, uninspired space and had created a lush fine-dining oasis.

Unease joined the admiration cruising around in him, creating a strange brew of emotions in his mind. Maybe it was going to be harder to compete against her than he'd thought.

Before the apprehension had a chance to grow, he spotted Jill walking down a hall toward him. She looked as fresh and pretty as always, dressed in a casual pair of navy blue pants and a clingy, short-sleeved white sweater. Her curves were emphasized in a way that called to every shred of healthy male in him. She had her golden hair pulled back in a clip at the base of her head, showing off the delicate bone structure of her face and her astonishingly blue eyes.

"Hey, Brandon," she said with a tentative but unmistakable smile.

So she wasn't going to show him the door—at least not yet.

She shifted her weight. "Um…what can I do for you?"

"I need to talk to you about the girls."

"Is something wrong?" she asked, her brow knitted.

"No, no, of course not." He gave her a rueful smile. "At least, nothing beyond their desperate attempts to get us together."

She nodded slowly and looked at her watch. After a long pause, she said, "You have good timing. The lunch crowd has thinned out enough that I can take a break."

"Then can we sit down and talk over lunch?"

"Here?"

He lifted one shoulder. "Why not?"

She paused. "Yes, why not." She gestured to the plant-filled dining room. "Why don't we sit down?"

"I'd like that."

He held his arm out for her to go first, then followed her to a small table close to the front desk. Before she could do it herself, he pulled out her chair for her.

She gave him an awkward little smile and sat. He moved around to the opposite side of the table and lowered himself into the other chair.

He picked up the menu, perusing the layout and graphics—very nice—and selections. The lunch choices ranged from gourmet burgers and sand-wiches to light grilled fish and meat entrées to meal-sized salads. She featured only one steak item, a good thing for him, and in general, the food was lighter and a little more eclectic than the lunch menu he had planned. He had to admit, though, that all of the items were very well presented and sounded delicious.

That certainly didn't bode well for him.

After he'd spent a few minutes looking over the entire menu, he looked up and noticed Jill peering at him, her eyes slightly narrowed. Guilt ate at him. Did she have any idea he was here to scope out her restaurant?

He cleared his throat. "This all looks great," he said, keeping his voice even. "What do you suggest?"

She arched one blond brow and stared at him for a long moment. "The wasabi grilled halibut is good today, as is the grilled chicken Caesar salad. Actually, Mr. Clark, everything is pretty good today."

"I have no doubt that all of the food you serve is delicious," he said, loosening his collar a bit. "Halibut sounds great. I'll have that."

"Excellent choice." She took a big swig of water. "So what's up with the girls?"

He shrugged. "Maybe nothing. But I have the impression they're planning something. Something big. Kris has been skulking around for the last few days, looking really guilty."

Jill's eyes flashed. "Darn them. I had a long, serious talk with Zoe the other day and told her to stop, and she acted like she understood." She let out a derisive snort under her breath. "I should have known better."

"I had the same discussion with Kristy, and even though she acted kind of mad that I wasn't going to sweep you off your feet anytime soon, I thought she got the message."

Jill rolled her eyes and shook her head. "Honestly—"

Her reply was interrupted by the arrival of their waitress, a round young woman sporting a name tag that said "Rachel."

"What can I get for you two?" she asked, her mouth pressed into a pleased smile, her eyes darting back and forth between him and Jill. Was there some private joke between her and Jill that he wasn't in on? One involving poisoning the competition, maybe?

Jill glared daggers at Rachel. "Two orders of the wasabi grilled halibut, please."

"Coming right up," Rachel said as she headed toward the kitchen, still smiling, her eyes sparkling.

Jill leaned back in her chair and rolled her eyes. "Oh, brother."

"What was that all about?"

"Nothing more than overly nosy, manipulating minds at work."

"Meaning?"

She drank a few more swallows of water and put the glass down with a *thunk*. "Meaning I mentioned to my manager that you and I had spent some time together, and now everyone in this place apparently thinks you and I are an item."

He fought to keep his jaw from dropping. "Even though I'm your...competitor?"

"Hey, what can I say? I work with a couple of romantics who don't get that the fact that you and I are competitors is pretty much relationship poison."

Relationship poison.

"Those are some pretty harsh words," he said, even as he belatedly realized that what she'd said was dead-on. Their antagonistic business relationship made any kind of personal connection unlikely, if not impossible. Funny how a pair of blue, blue eyes, a beautiful smile and a sad story about gaining respect had made him forget that.

"Harsh, but true, and I can't afford to think any other way." She skewered him with a calculating look. "For all I know, you're really here to check out the competition."

More acidic guilt exploded inside him. "I'll admit, I am interested in how you run your business. But I did want to give you a heads-up about the girls, too."

"You could have done that over the phone," she said, her voice edged with steel, her eyes as hard as sapphires. "Right?"

She had his number, big-time. Man, she was sharp. One more thing to admire, one more reason to be really worried about whether he was going to emerge victorious in the restaurant game or flop miserably.

He shifted in his chair. He might be a tad sneaky, but he wasn't a liar. "Touché," he said, holding up his water glass. "You've got me there. I guess I wanted to know what I was up against."

Her eyes flashed and she leaned forward, her shoulders rigid. "So you're admitting—"

Her reply was cut off by an elderly man two tables over, shouting his order for grilled chicken at Rachel.

Jill caught Brandon's eye. "Mr. Hobbs," she said, inclining her head toward the gray-haired gentleman, smiling indulgently. "He's a little hard of hearing."

Brandon nodded, liking how she graciously tolerated the man's disturbingly loud voice. Her graciousness made him cringe inside. "I should have been honest with you from the start about why I was here," he said. "I'm sorry I wasn't."

She stared at him for a long time while she tapped one index finger on the table. After a few seconds of awkward silence, her shoulders relaxed. "Well…it does kind of make me mad you came here with an ulterior motive. But as long as we're being honest, I'll admit that I tried to look in the windows of your place today. The paper you've put up kept me from seeing anything, but I tried." Her lips curved into a small, sheepish smile. "So I guess we're even."

He let out a breath of relief, glad she hadn't asked him to leave. Though it was crazy, he enjoyed her company. And he had to admit he was really looking forward to his lunch, and not just because it would give him a clue as to how good her chef really was. He was starving.

Their food arrived and Brandon devoured his delicious grilled halibut, stir-fried veggies and rice pilaf. He noted that Jill just picked at her halibut, even though the dish was cooked to perfection.

As they ate they discussed inane subjects like the weather and their favorite TV shows. Inevitably, the conversation then turned to Kristy and Zoe's continued matchmaking maneuvers. Jill agreed with Brandon that their plan to "play along" wasn't working. They decided that both would again have very stern conversations with their daughters, making it clear to the girls that major punishment involving grounding and loss of privileges—including playtime with each other—would result if Kristy and Zoe didn't cooperate.

A few minutes later their intense conversation was interrupted by the loud voice of Mr. Hobbs. "That's not what I ordered, missy. Take it back."

Jill's attention immediately veered to Mr. Hobbs.

"Mr. Hobbs," Rachel said in a very patient voice considering the old man had indeed ordered chicken loudly enough for the people across Main Street to hear, "you very specifically ordered the grilled quarter chicken." She pulled out her order pad. "See here? I wrote it down."

"I don't care what you have written down." He waved a hand in the air, then crossed his thin arms over his chest. "I hate chicken and would never have ordered it."

Jill rose, putting her napkin on the table, and headed to Mr. Hobbs's table. "No problem, Mr. Hobbs," she said in a soothing voice. "What would you like to have?"

He gave Rachel a smug smile. "I want the steak," he told Jill. "Medium rare."

She looked at Rachel. "Please get Mr. Hobbs the grilled New York steak, Rachel. And add a slice of apple pie to his order, gratis, please. I know that's his favorite."

Jill patted Mr. Hobbs's bony shoulder. "Will that be all right, Mr. Hobbs?"

He nodded. "Just fine, Jill. Only a fine eating establishment takes care of its customers like you do. That's why I come here, you know."

"I know. And I appreciate your business, really I do."

Awed to the core by Jill's diplomatic handling of Mr. Hobbs's cantankerous behavior, Brandon shifted his gaze to Rachel. She rolled her eyes, but to her credit, remained silent and went to the kitchen as instructed.

Jill returned to the table and sat. "Rachel usually works the evening shift and isn't familiar with Mr. Hobbs's lunchtime antics."

"You handled that very well. I'm very impressed."

Her cheeks colored. "Really?"

He leaned in and covered her hand with his. "Really. You kept a regular customer happy, even when he was wrong. Smart move." He looked around. "In fact, I'm impressed by everything about this place. You've done a wonderful job, Jill. Really spectacular. To be honest, you've actually got me worried. I really respect you as honest competition."

She smiled, her face literally glowing with obvious pride. "Thank you. I've worked very hard to make this restaurant successful."

Brandon looked into her sparkling South Sea eyes, and she stared back. His breath left him in a heated rush and he felt the pull of her clear down to his toes. A warm glow settled in the center of his chest, heating him from the inside out.

Another employee approached the table and asked Jill to come to the kitchen to handle a problem, breaking the spell. Her cheeks still in high color, Jill graciously agreed, rose and left him sitting alone.

He watched her go, his gaze encompassing The Grill with its soothing fountain and richly hued, inviting decor and oasis-like ambience. He recalled what a pro she'd been handling crotchety old Mr. Hobbs, who had probably been angling for a free dessert all along. He looked at his clean plate, admitting that the food she served was of the highest caliber.

She was something, all right. She was genuine business competition. And that added up to one very bad thing.

He could easily be the one to skulk out of town, an unemployed, total failure, his dreams going up in flames.

But he couldn't help the fact that he admired Jill. Respected her. Liked her. A lot.

And that was going to make it damn hard to go

all out to make his restaurant the place to eat in Elm Corners. His success would undoubtedly affect Jill's business goals, goals she'd been working toward for years. For very good, very personally significant reasons. After a lifetime of being the daughter of the town goof, she wanted the town's respect.

Was he prepared to be the one to take that away from her?

Did he have a choice?

Jill handled the problem in the kitchen, then headed back out to the dining room, still glowing with a kind of warm, spine-tingling pride that stretched into the furthest recesses of her battered self-esteem.

Brandon was impressed by her. He respected her. *Wow.* Who would have thought that hearing him say those things would make her so darn happy?

But he had made her happy. And she liked the feeling. More than she should.

Brandon stood by the front desk. As she approached him, she couldn't help but admire all over again how attractive he looked in a pair of well-fitting navy blue khakis and a cream button-down shirt that emphasized his dark eyes and olive-toned skin.

Excitement and pleasure hit her all at once. She honestly had to say she couldn't find one thing she didn't like about him. Not one thing.

Well, except the irritating detail that he was the owner of The Steak Place...

"I already paid the bill," he said, a vague shadow in his eyes.

She frowned. "I own the place. Lunch was on me, silly."

"No, no," he said. "I wanted to pay my own way, since you were gracious enough to have lunch with me."

"I won't argue, all right?" she said. He was too stubborn to change his mind. "Next time, though, it'll be my treat." She forced a smile. "Although there won't be a next time, will there?"

What looked like regret burned in his eyes. "No, I guess not. Well, I have a meeting across town in ten minutes." He turned to leave. "Thanks again for your time. I really had a nice time, and the lunch was delicious."

Wanting to keep that warm glow alive as well as thank him for being so appreciative of her hard work, she followed him out the door. "I'll walk out with you."

She kept pace with him to his vehicle parked in the small lot next to The Grill.

"Listen, Brandon," she said when they reached his SUV, "I want to tell you something."

He stopped and looked at her, his jaw softening just a bit. "What is it?"

Acting on the warm fuzzies swirling inside her, she stepped closer and touched his arm. "I wanted to thank you for what you said in there. Your respect means a lot to me."

He stilled, then moved toward her, bringing them

so close her heart started racing. "I meant everything I said," he said in a low, husky voice that made her knees feel like warm pudding. "You impress the hell out of me."

His words were a soothing balm to her wounded soul. Her eyes suddenly burning, she looked up at him, noting the flecks of black in his dark brown eyes, wanting to lose herself in his gaze. "Nobody has ever said that to me."

His eyes roamed her face, then he touched her cheek. "Then they were fools," he whispered, his voice a husky rasp across her wounded heart. "You're one of the most amazing women I've ever met."

A tight, hard knot somewhere inside her slowly unfurled, loosening the tightness in her chest, bringing her a long-forgotten contentment and joy.

He thought she was amazing.

She smiled at him, looking deep into his eyes, unable to speak around the lump in her throat.

His hand moved from her cheek to sweep her hair back from her face, his touch like fire. "You are so beautiful," he murmured, his breath hot on her face, pressing a kiss to her forehead.

Jill moaned, loving the rasp of his whiskers on her face and how his hard, well-muscled body felt like warm steel. Dizzy with need, filled with the warm glow his admiration had caused, wanting more—so much more—she lifted her face and pressed her mouth to his.

Brandon let out a low groan, then wrapped his arms around her and kissed her back, his mouth hot and hard on her lips.

Breathless and on fire and shaky all at once, Jill wrapped her arms around his waist and burrowed closer, kissing him back with everything in her. Lost in Brandon, she felt her sanity float away on the leaf-rustling breeze. A profound sense of belonging settled around her, soothing and comforting her in a way nothing had in a very long time.

His scent surrounded her, a combination of soap, aftershave and fresh air, making her dizzy with long-forgotten desire. She pressed her hands against his broad, well-muscled back, loving the masculine feel of him, loving how his lips caressed hers. She wished the world would disappear and she could stay here forever, safe and secure in his arms, a whole, competent person, the autumn sun warming them until they melted together and became one.

Needing to catch her breath, she pulled back slightly, breaking their sizzling kiss. Trembling, she stared into burnt-caramel eyes glowing with undisguised desire.

Her heart stuttered and sheer excitement pulsed through her veins, hot and druglike, chasing away the remains of her sanity. It had been so long since she'd been close to a man like this. So long since she'd been made to feel so wanted, so special. How easy it would be to lose herself completely in him, to pull his head down and kiss him all day long.

Weak with longing, she stood on her tiptoes and moved her hands to his shoulders. "Brandon," she breathed, pulling on him, wanting another kiss more than her next breath. Smiling, Brandon obliged, bending his head…

A car's horn honked nearby. She froze a few inches from his lips, her common sense gushing back into her.

What am I doing?

Shaking, she yanked her hands from his broad shoulders and extricated herself from his warm, sheltering arms, feeling the loss like a cold stone in her heart. Suddenly chilled, she stepped back and away from him, touching her tingling lips with a quivering hand.

"Jill," he said, following her. "Don't…"

Her hand still pressed to her mouth, she shook her head. "I have to." She sucked in a calming breath. "I'm not exactly thinking clearly at the moment."

He looked up at the sky. "I know the feeling."

Subduing her need to invite him closer for another knee-weakening kiss, she took a deep breath, steeling her flustered self for a serious, obviously much-needed heart-to-heart.

"Brandon," she said, gesturing between them, "this was a mistake. I should never have kissed you."

He looked at her for a long time, his eyebrows raised high, his dark eyes reflecting conflict.

When he didn't respond, she continued. "Obviously we're, uh…well, attracted to one another."

"You've got that right. I like you a lot, and I

respect and admire you, too." He scrubbed his face with his hand. "Maybe too much."

While his words flattered her, she had to be smart here. And smart meant putting a quick and heavy lid on the way they were drawn to each other. "I wish our mutual attraction could lead somewhere—"

"But it can't, right?" Even as he said the words, he moved closer, too close, his eyes moving over her in a way that lit tiny fires underneath every inch of her skin. Couple that with how much she liked and respected him, and...well, it would be so darn easy to jump into something she just wasn't ready for.

She consciously stepped back so she could think clearly and so she wouldn't fling herself into his arms and kiss him until he begged for mercy. "Right," she whispered. "You're my competition. I can't let myself forget that."

"I know you're being smart, but at this moment it's all I can do not to kiss you all over again," he said, his voice low, husky and so darned sexy she almost melted into a pool of mush right there.

Something throbbed inside her—something sexual, yes, but also something lonely and needy and so desperate for attention since Doug had made her feel so useless, so disposable.

So unworthy.

"It would be easy to give in to my attraction to you," she said, shaking her head. "I haven't had any positive attention from a man for a very long time."

"Again, I find that hard to believe." He reached

out and stroked a finger down her cheek once more, his eyes hot on her face. "If you were mine, I'd give you more positive attention than you'd know what to do with."

She stared at him, her heart expanding until her chest felt stuffed full. Complete. The trail of fire his touch left on her cheek throbbed in time with the heat low in her belly. Oh, how she wanted to give in to her desire to be close to him, to bask in the wonderful way he made her feel. Loved. Wanted. Perfect.

But her scarred heart and her common sense wouldn't let her go to that place. Not even for the perfect man—Brandon. She had to stop this right here, right now, before she did something stupid.

She had to tell him why, had to make him understand. As much for his sake as for hers. "I have a lot of reasons to stay away from you. Of course, the first is that I would be an idiot to let myself get close to someone who could ruin my business." She drew in a deep, calming breath. "Second, my ex hurt me a lot, and left me feeling vulnerable and unworthy and so cut up inside I didn't think I'd get over it. I can't ever go through that kind of betrayal again." She paced away, her arms wrapped around her waist to keep herself warm. "I need to keep my distance from love."

"I'm not your ex. I'm not like that. I wouldn't ever hurt you," he said, his tone hard. He was obviously offended by what she'd implied.

"Maybe not intentionally," she said softly. "But

relationships by their nature are risky. You said yourself you never want to go through losing someone again, right?"

He let out a heavy breath. "Yeah, I said that, and I meant it."

"Well then, there you go. You don't want the risk, either." She tightened her jaw. And her heart. "We need to stay away from each other."

He looked at the pavement. "Even though a kiss doesn't equal a relationship, I acknowledge that we made a mistake." He lifted his head and smiled at her ruefully, his eyes crinkling at the corners. "We've spent a lot of time together talking, and I've gotten to know you. You're a great person, Jill. I guess I got a little carried away."

Her heart glowed, but she doused it. "The truth is, I'm scared to death any man I allow into my heart will leave me all alone down the road."

He caught her gaze and held it, seeing, it seemed, clear down to her soul. "Trust me, if I had you in my life, I'd never walk away from you." He quirked a tight grin. "Hypothetically, of course."

Even though he was speaking in ifs, her chest tightened for what she had to turn her back on, what she had to sacrifice to keep her heart—and business—safe and whole and healthy.

"You say that—hypothetically—you wouldn't walk away, but how would I be sure?" she asked, her voice tinged with sadness. "After all, you pulled up stakes and moved to Elm Corners for

Kristy. What would stop you from moving on when she's older?"

"What would keep you from coming with me?" he asked, a dark challenge in his eyes. "Theoretically, of course."

She rose to that challenge. "I have a business here that I've worked hard to build. That would certainly keep me here. Besides, maybe you wouldn't want me to go with you," she stated baldly. Doug certainly hadn't. Oh, no. He'd thrown her away like garbage and had already had another woman waiting in the wings when he walked away.

Brandon quickly moved into her space and took her hand in his. Leaning close, he whispered in her ear, "Trust me when I say that if things were different and I had your heart in my keeping, I'd never, ever want to be without you."

His breath raised more hot chills on her skin and his words reignited an intense yearning deep within.

A yearning she couldn't give in to. Life had taught her she couldn't believe in love ever again. She had to ignore what he made her want—happiness, caring, a beautiful forever after—and protect herself and all that she'd worked so hard for. She simply couldn't be put through the wringer again.

Steeling herself, she pulled away, breaking their connection. "You're talking about fantasies and dreams, Brandon, not something that could ever come true. You were hurt by love, too, even more than I was. You certainly don't want to put yourself in a situation that might lead to more pain."

He drew in a heavy breath and let it out, then looked at her, his eyes filled with a resigned sorrow that tugged at her heart. "No, you're right. I don't."

"Precisely," she said crisply, hiding the unexpected sadness she felt. "This discussion, while…interesting, is a waste of time."

He looked at her for a long moment. "I guess you're right," he said, checking his watch. "And I've got a meeting to get to. Thanks for your time." Without another word, he unlocked his car, got in and drove away.

Jill watched him leave, her throat burning, suddenly feeling empty. Alone. Hollow.

But nothing could change the fact that she and Brandon had no future. Ever.

Deep in her soul an emotion throbbed like an open wound. To her horror that emotion wasn't the relief she wanted to feel.

It was horrible, slicing regret.

Chapter Eight

After handling another heavy lunch crowd, Jill stood at the front desk of The Grill midday, gathering the receipts. She heard the main door open and looked up expecting to see Fred, their regular mail carrier.

Her breath stalled in her throat. Brandon, whom she hadn't seen for two days since they'd had lunch and kissed, stepped through the door. His dark hair looked disheveled as if he'd jammed his fingers through it, and his eyes were darkened by deep concern.

Her stomach dropped. "What's wrong?" She hastily came out from behind the counter, instinctively sensing he wasn't there with good news.

"I came to work late today and found this letter on my desk at the restaurant," he replied, holding up a white piece of paper.

With shaking hands she took the letter from him and looked at the neat, computer-printed note.

Dear Mom and Dad:
    We are hiding somewhere and you need to work together to find us. Go to Kristy's house for the next clue.
    Zoe and Kristy

She looked at Brandon, rolling her eyes. "Oh, brother. These two never quit, do they?"

"They're very determined." He folded the note and shoved it in his pants pocket. "I knew they were up to something."

A niggle of concern pinched at her. "Other than being irritating, this is no big deal. They'll be okay, right?"

Brandon stepped closer and laid his warm hands on her shoulders, squeezing. "The note didn't sound particularly threatening. We'll find them quickly, I'm sure."

Her worry eased at his touch. "I can't believe they pulled this kind of stunt, just to get us together."

"Me, neither," he said, rubbing her upper arms in a way that calmed her even as a tingly warmth spread through her.

"So what are we going to do?"

He lifted one broad shoulder. "We're going to follow the clues as instructed, and when we find them, there's going to be hell to pay."

Thankful for Brandon's levelheaded presence, Jill stepped away from him and rushed into the kitchen to let Mel know she was leaving, while Brandon pulled his SUV to the front entrance of The Grill. She hustled to her office and grabbed her purse.

Jill left the building less than a minute later and jumped into the passenger seat of his SUV. Her hands gripped in a knot in her lap, she leaned back in the leather passenger seat and tried to relax as Brandon peeled out.

"I'm going to call my dad and see if he knows where the girls are." She dug in her purse for her phone. "I'll string him up if he had anything to do with this."

She quickly dialed his home number, but there was no answer. Uttering an oath, she punched in his cell phone number, but it went directly to his voice mail.

"Darn it," she exclaimed, pressing the red button hard. "I gave him that cell phone so I could reach him in emergencies. I wish he'd charge the thing once in a while."

She remained silent for the rest of the five-minute trip to Brandon's house, too irritated to say much. She simply couldn't believe that the girls would send them on a ridiculous wild-goose chase after they'd both been told numerous times to stop their meddling.

Zoe was in big, big trouble.

They arrived at Brandon's house in record time. She had never been there, since her dad always picked up Zoe. She noted that Brandon's residence was a pleasant, older ranch-style home painted dark green, located on a large lot in a cul-de-sac studded with towering oak and elm trees.

She hopped out of the car and followed him inside. They entered a small, tiled foyer, then walked through a large, uncluttered living room furnished with tasteful dark leather couches, dust-free oak furniture and a gigantic big-screen TV. The carpet looked freshly vacuumed.

Brandon headed into the spacious kitchen, which sported sparkling oak cabinets, shiny hardwood floors, gleaming stainless steel appliances—the fridge was covered in Kristy's artwork—and pristine-looking beige tile countertops.

Jill smiled, holding in a gasp of surprise. The place was spotlessly clean with everything in its place, all the way down to the sponge that sat in its own little holder on the side of the sink.

Obviously Brandon was one tidy guy.

Another note sat front and center on the kitchen counter.

"I wondered why Kristy had to run back in here this morning," he muttered.

Jill picked up the note and unfolded it. Brandon stood in back of her and read it over her shoulder.

Mom and Dad:

   Kristy hid a note in her dad's office at The Steak Place. Go there for your next clue.

   Zoe and Kristy

Brandon swore and pounded the counter. "This is ridiculous. I was just there."

Jill sighed. "Well, let's get going. The sooner we find them, the better. How complicated could they make this, anyway?" She held on to that thought like a lifeline as they hightailed it back out to Brandon's vehicle. She just wanted to find the girls and be done with this gigantic waste of time. She hated being manipulated, especially since they'd told the girls so many times to stop.

He retraced his route back to The Steak Place, driving just as fast as he had going the opposite way. When they arrived back on Main Street, he parked the car in an open space on the street in front of his restaurant.

Jill followed him into The Steak Place, anticipation bubbling like mad inside her. She was finally going to get a look at what was going on behind the paper-covered windows.

The large space was in the middle of renovations that had turned the future restaurant into a cluttered, scaffold-strewn mess. Several men were working on the dark wooden flooring while two others were installing leather-lined booths. A couple workers at the back of the space looked to be painting the walls a rich shade of terra-cotta. The place looked as if it was shaping up to be a very high-class endeavor.

Jill ignored the shudder of trepidation that shot through her—he was concrete, do-or-die competition now—and followed Brandon down a narrow hallway to a small room at the back of the restaurant. She dogged his heels. This letter had better be the last one.

She wanted to find Zoe and ground her for the next ten years.

"They said the letter was hidden here," he said, casting his gaze around the small yet scrupulously neat office, which looked as if it wasn't being remodeled at this time. The white-walled room was dominated by a large wooden desk and leather office chair and nothing else.

Jill looked around for an obvious hiding place, but due to the lack of furniture, the choices were few. The letter had to be hidden in his desk. Acting on instinct, she went over to the desk.

Brandon met her there and pulled the top drawer open.

The letter lay there on top of a couple pens. Thank goodness they were dealing with two young kids instead of some really resourceful, clever teenagers.

He pulled the letter out and held it up. "Bingo."

Brandon unfolded the letter and held it out so they could both read it.

Dear Mom and Dad:
Go to the Lindstroms' house for the next clue.
Zoe and Kristy

"I'm going to wring her neck," Jill muttered.

He crumpled the letter into a ball. "We can have a party and do it together," he said, sharply gesturing to the door. "Let's go."

Feeling like a puppet on a string, Jill headed back down the hall and to his car, worry beginning to eat a hole in her belly. "If they're not at my house, where else could they be?" she asked over her shoulder, anxiety flaring. "What if they're wandering around town by themselves?"

Brandon caught her hand to stop her.

She did, then turned and looked at him, biting her lower lip.

"Jill," he said gently, taking both of her shaking hands in his, "this is a small town, and everybody knows the girls. Nothing bad is going to happen to them, all right?"

She nodded, her heart squeezing, thankful he was by her side at a time like this. She was deeply grateful for his rock-solid presence and ability to stay level-headed when her overactive, motherly imagination was starting to work overtime.

As they drove to her house, she wondered what she would do if he weren't here to keep her calm. Though her first priority was to find the girls, she allowed her mind to wander to Brandon and his growing importance in her life.

She couldn't help but admit that he was everything she could possibly want in a man.

If she wanted a man.

She hadn't wanted to take that risk since Doug had hurt her so badly, but Brandon…well, despite the risks he posed to her, he'd worked his way into her heart with his gentleness, sense of humor and devotion to Kristy.

She let out a shaky sigh. Trust her funky soul to go haywire in the middle of a major crisis that had yet to be resolved. She had to concentrate on finding the girls, not on her frightening feelings for the man by her side.

Shoving her surprising thoughts to the back of her mind, she focused on the here and now—locating the girls.

There would be plenty of time after the neck-wringing party to decide what to do about her new feelings for Brandon.

Brandon pulled into Jill's driveway and shoved the SUV into Park. Setting his jaw, he hopped out of the vehicle. The girls had better be here.

They'd crossed a line with this stunt, and it was time for the whole thing to be over and done with.

For good.

He followed Jill into the house and down the hall to the kitchen as she tersely called for the girls. No answer.

Another letter lay on the counter. Jill snatched it up and unfolded it. They both read in silence.

Dear Mom and Dad:
    We're at Grandpa's house.
    Kristy and Zoe

Damn. A short, sweet letter that irritated him no end. He didn't like having his chain yanked by two precocious kids. Thankfully, though, they'd found the girls.

Burning relief spread through him.

Jill let out a disgusted sound. "I should have known that's where they were," she said, smashing the letter. "It's Zoe's safe haven." After she pitched the ball of paper across the room, she stomped across the kitchen to the back door. "Come on. It's neck-wringing time."

He silently followed her out the door, acknowledging that she was totally justified in her attitude, owning a corner of parental disgust over what the girls had done.

Apparently in high fury, Jill stormed ahead of him, her chin in the air, and rushed across the grass to the garage, her golden hair flying. She clomped up the outside staircase to the apartment over the garage, then flung open the door without knocking.

"You two naughty girls better be here," she shouted. "Get out here, Zoe. Now."

Brandon stepped into her dad's apartment and

looked around, noting a small, cluttered front room/kitchen area decorated in bland colors and older-style furniture. What looked to be odd inventions made out of wood, metal and wire sat all about the room and piles of magazines lined the walls.

Zoe and Kristy came out from a short hallway at the back of the living room. "You found us!" Zoe exclaimed, smiling. "Good job."

Jill hurried over to the girls, then pulled both of them close, her relief obviously taking precedence over her anger. "I was worried about you two."

Brandon moved to join the hugging fray, but a familiar item on the coffee table in front of the couch caught his eye. Frowning, he moved closer and saw something very strange.

His wedding album lay open on the low table, his and Sandy's smiling faces looking back at him. Next to it lay another album, open to a close-up picture of a younger-looking Jill in a white wedding veil smiling lovingly at a man who had sandy-blond hair.

His stomach knotted. What was all this?

First things first. He dragged his attention away from the albums, walked over to Kristy and put a heavy hand on her shoulder. "You pulled a stupid stunt," he said, infusing just enough anger into his voice to make a point.

Kristy pulled away and looked up at him, her brown eyes full of worry. "Are you mad?"

"Of course I am, Kris," he said, his lips barely moving. No way was he going to cut her any slack.

"You manipulated us after we specifically told you to stop."

She blinked away tears. "I knew you would be mad, but Zoe and I want a family real bad, and this was our last plan."

"Still," Jill said, her mouth firm and unyielding, "you girls shouldn't have done something like this. You know that, don't you?"

Both girls nodded.

Before Jill could go on, Brandon picked up his wedding album and held it up. "While I think this conversation is important, Jill, I think you and I have some other things to talk about."

She looked over at him, her expression questioning. Slowly she walked to the coffee table. She let out a gasp when she saw her own wedding album on the table.

She turned disbelieving eyes on her daughter. "Zoe, did you put these here?" she asked in a quiet, low voice.

Zoe bobbed her head.

"Why?" Jill asked.

"I thought maybe if you remembered how happy you and Daddy were when you got married you'd want to get married again. To Mr. Clark."

Jill looked stricken.

But before she could reply, Mr. Winters hurried through the door, his wild gray hair flying around his head as usual, a bag of groceries in his arms. He stopped in his tracks when he saw everyone standing in his small living room.

"What's going on?" he asked, raising his bushy eyebrows, looking from Jill to Brandon and back again.

In a brusque voice Jill explained what the girls had done. When she was through, she walked over to her father. "You didn't have anything to do with any of this, did you?"

"Of course not," he said, glowering. "I would never help the girls do anything like that."

Jill pointed to the albums. "I have that album…in a place Zoe can't reach." She swallowed. "Did you get it out for her?"

"Yes, I did. She said she wanted to look at it, because she liked seeing you and her father together all dressed up in your wedding clothes."

Jill nodded mutely, wringing her hands, her jaw rigid. She looked as if she didn't know what to say, as if she was slightly shell-shocked.

Brandon stepped forward, concern for Jill running rampant in him. "Mr. Winters, would you mind taking the girls into the house and getting them a snack? I think Jill and I need to have a talk."

"Sure thing, Brandon."

He put the grocery bag down on the floor and hustled the girls to the door. Before they left, Brandon said in a steely voice, "Kristy, this isn't the end of the discussion about what you've done, or what your punishment will be, do you understand?"

Kristy nodded.

"Same goes for you, Zoe," Jill added. "We'll talk later."

Mr. Winters and the girls left, leaving Brandon alone with Jill.

And their wedding albums.

Jill stayed quiet as she moved over and picked up her album, staring at the picture.

Brandon let her look without speaking, and took the opportunity to look at his own wedding pictures, something he hadn't been able to do since his wife had died. Call it weak, but he'd feared and dreaded the emotions seeing the photos of his wedding—the happiest day of his life so far—would cause.

He couldn't help but look at Sandy, glowing as a bride. He grimly prepared himself for the grinding, shattering pain of his grief.

His breath stalled in his throat. Strangely, all he felt was a profound sadness that he had lost someone he loved deeply. As he stared at Sandy with her dark hair and eyes and beautiful smile so like Kristy, he remembered the happiness he'd found with his wife, how head over heels in love he'd been with her and how that love had been the best thing that had ever happened to him.

Then an overpowering thought hit him. He missed that kind of happiness, the kind that came only with having a special woman in his life. He missed looking into a woman's eyes and feeling connected to her soul. He missed holding a woman in his arms, kissing and making love to her and lying together afterward in the dark, talking. He missed coming home and having dinner with the woman he loved, holding hands under the table and cleaning up together after the meal, joking and laughing.

He missed all of it. Desperately.

And he wanted that feeling again, wanted the security and sense of belonging and elation only romantic love caused.

Despite the risk to his heart.

Stunned—no, elated—he looked at Jill sitting on the couch, staring at the album in her hands, her shoulders curved inward.

Suddenly everything was so clear. He loved her. He wanted her in his life, wanted to feel alive and happy and contented again. He wanted all of the things he was missing. With her. Because of her.

He opened his mouth to tell her, but stopped when she glanced up at him, tears tumbling down her pale cheeks.

She held up the wedding album and pointed to the photo of her ex-husband. "This is why I can never be with you," she said, her voice hollow.

His heart crumbled. "So you still love him?"

She laughed harshly, dashing the tears from her cheeks. "No, of course not. But these pictures are the proof of my lost happiness, of my pain and Doug's betrayal. He didn't respect me and thought of me as nothing more than a boring housewife, then dumped me when someone better came along." She slammed the album closed and gripped its edges with white-knuckled fingers. "I've said it before, and I'll say it one more time. I can never put myself into a position to let a man stomp all over me again."

Brandon stared at her, his chest filled with a searing ache. He wanted to tell her that he was different, that he loved her too much to ever hurt her. But he'd already essentially told her that, and it hadn't made any difference. Jill had been hurt and she couldn't get around that. Not even for him or the love they could share.

The ache inside him grew until he could barely breathe. Powerless in the face of her heart-paralyzing fears, he watched his chance for happiness flit away, cut down before he could even tell her that he loved her.

He ground his teeth, shoving the pain away. Hey, he'd had his epiphany after looking at his wedding pictures. And obviously, she'd had hers. Too damn bad his wake-up call had shown him love and hers had driven it away.

A bone-deep sense of loss filled him, a searing hurt that radiated outward into every inch of his body.

Leave. He had to leave, had to get out of there and lick his wounds, away from lost dreams and unrequited love and Jill's inability to forget her past. "Uh…well, I'd better go and…talk to Kristy." He moved to the door. "I'll see you later."

Before she could stop him—not that she would, anyway—he stepped outside, struggling to breathe.

He'd been a fool to fall for a woman who would

never be able to set aside the pain in her past and love him.

At least he'd figured out that fateful truth before he'd made an even bigger joke of himself by actually telling Jill how he felt.

Even so, he found no comfort there.

He'd lost the woman he loved. Again.

Chapter Nine

Jill thanked a customer, then answered the ringing phone. "Wildflower Grill. How can I help you?"

"Is Jill Lindstrom available?"

"This is Jill."

"Jill, this is Marge from the drugstore. I hate to be the one to deliver bad news, but your father collapsed here about ten minutes ago, and they've taken him to the hospital."

Ice water ran through Jill's veins. "Is he…okay?"

"He's alive, but CPR was involved, so it was serious, maybe a heart attack." Marge softened her voice. "I'd get to the hospital as fast as you can."

"Thank you for calling," she said, then hung up the phone with shaking hands. Near panic, she ran to the kitchen, told Mel she was leaving and why, then hurried to her car.

Her hands stiff on the steering wheel, she drove to the hospital, making an effort not to speed, but failing. Dear heaven, all she could think about was that her dad was getting up in years and had collapsed and might not make it.

Barely able to breathe, she wheeled into the hospital parking lot, found a parking space and rushed into the three-story brick building. After asking at the information desk what room her father was in, she hustled to the cardiac unit on the third floor.

She pushed open the swinging door and stepped into room 405, her heart pounding in dread, her hand clamped like a vise around her purse strap.

As pale as a ghost and his hair sticking straight up as usual, her father lay in the large hospital bed before her. Somehow he appeared small and helpless despite being a tall, robust, barrel-chested man.

Her eyes burned and tears squeezed out to run down her cheeks as she struggled for control. She didn't know what she'd do if she lost him. She had no other family except Zoe. Without her dad…well, she couldn't begin to fathom life without him.

She was glad to see Dr. Samuel Phelps in the room. Though they didn't travel in the same social circles, Elm Corners was a small town, and she knew of him and his impeccable professional reputation. He was an extremely well-respected cardiologist, and a pillar in the Elm Corners community. "Dr. Phelps." She turned her gaze to her dad. "How is he?"

Dr. Phelps inclined his head to the side, his gray eyes thoughtful. "Stable now, but he did have a life-threatening heart attack, apparently at the drugstore this morning. Someone called 911 while a clerk performed CPR." He tapped the clipboard with his pen. "Probably saved his life."

Her chest tight, Jill nodded and moved closer to her dad. Seeing such a vital man strung out in a hospital bed twisted her insides into knots. "Is he going to be okay?" she asked, wiping the tears from her cheeks.

"He's going to have to make some changes in his lifestyle—a healthy diet and daily exercise are key, plus heart medication for the rest of his life. But if he does all that, he should be okay."

"He does love sweets and fattening food," she said, giving the doctor a wry smile. "I guess those days are over."

Dr. Phelps lifted one corner of his mouth. "Yes, I remember how much he liked ice cream with hot fudge and whipped cream."

Jill drew her eyebrows together. "You do?"

"Yes, I do," he said, nodding. "We went to med school together."

Jill almost swallowed her tongue. *Med school?* "Wh-what?"

"Yes, all four years. We were even roommates a couple of those years. I was with him the night he met your mother." He gave her an odd look. "You didn't know that?"

Her knees shaking, Jill moved over and sank into the lone chair in the room, dropping her purse on the floor. "No. I—I had no idea my dad went to medical school." He'd been an inventor for her whole life, or at least as long as she remembered. A wacky inventor who embarrassed her. She cringed at the thought. Apparently there was more—much more—to her dad than she'd realized.

"That he did." Dr. Phelps smiled. "He was quite brilliant, in fact, the envy of everyone in our class. We used to joke that we'd have to get rid of him somehow because he always set the grading curve so high."

Before Jill could make her mouth work and form words, Dr. Phelps's beeper went off. He consulted it, then hung the clipboard at the base of the bed. "I'm needed in the O.R." He stepped closer and laid a hand on her shoulder. "I'll check back later today, all right? He'll sleep for a while, I'm sure."

Jill nodded absently, her gaze on her dad, her jaw slack. Dr. Phelps headed out of the hospital room, leaving Jill alone with her father, a huge lump forming in her throat. Questions about what she'd discovered clamored in her mind. Why hadn't he told her he'd almost become a doctor? Why hadn't he gone on and actually practiced medicine?

She shoved those questions aside for the moment, focusing instead on how grateful she was that her dad had survived and equally grateful to the Good Samaritans who'd taken care of him. She made a mental note to find out who they were and thank them personally.

She rose and went to the bed, taking her dad's large, age-spotted hand in hers. "I don't want to lose you, Dad." He'd been her only family for as long as she could remember. He'd braided her hair, stayed up with her when she'd been sick, supported her when she'd married Doug even though she suspected he'd known all along that Doug would break her heart, and had stood faithfully by her when Doug had ditched her. He'd also been a fantastic grandfather to her daughter and by taking care of Zoe had allowed Jill to pursue her dreams of opening a restaurant.

She allowed the tears to flow in earnest. Her dad was very ill and could die. He'd gone to medical school. She suddenly felt ashamed that she'd always been so resentful of his occupation. Especially now that she'd discovered the truth about him.

Looked as if her dad was full of surprises—and secrets.

She couldn't wait to talk to him about them. Maybe he'd forgive her for forgetting how important he was to her. If only she'd be able to forgive herself.

Stepping back, she gently let go of his hand so she could drag the chair closer. Weary yet keyed up and shaky, she sat in the chair and reclaimed her dad's hand.

She looked around the ugly, drab hospital room,

feeling alone and scared and desperately in need of a comforting shoulder to lean on.

Brandon's face popped into her mind. Yes, Brandon was the person she needed right now. She needed his strong arms around her, his calm levelheadedness, his loving, gentle concern and support.

She reached for her purse on the floor to dig out her cell phone to call him.

But her hand stopped midway, then fell limply at her side. She'd given in to her fears and told him she could never be with him, had literally thrown that darn wedding album in his face three days ago. She'd let him walk away from her.

She couldn't call Brandon and expect him to run over here and take care of her. Not after what she'd done.

No, she was on her own. As she'd always been. She'd have to get through this crisis by herself.

Her shoulders slumping and feeling more alone than ever, she laid her head down on the edge of her father's hospital bed and cried.

The day after her dad had his heart attack Jill walked into his hospital room at 9:00 a.m. Her mouth fell open. There were flowers, balloons and get-well cards filling the room.

Her jaw still sagging, she looked at her dad, relieved to see him sitting up in bed, wide-awake. While he was still a bit pale, most of his color had returned, and he looked almost as wild and woolly as he usually did.

A huge, crushing load was lifted off her shoulders. While Dr. Phelps had assured her yesterday that her dad was going to be okay, she'd still spent the whole day hovering by his side waiting for him to wake up, unable to stop her dire thoughts. What if he didn't wake up? What if he had another attack? What if she was left all alone except for Zoe, with absolutely no other relatives? Panicky fear had filled her, clogging her chest, bringing hot tears to the surface time and time again.

She'd also wished many times that Brandon was by her side, helping her through the crisis. But it wasn't to be. As the saying went, she'd made her bed. Now she needed to lie in it, even if it ripped her heart out and made her feel so alone she thought she'd never survive.

After a fear-filled, tortuous day, her dad had awakened in the late afternoon, feeling groggy but able to talk. While Jill had wanted to ask him about medical school, she'd held off. He needed to take it easy, and she certainly didn't want to have a conversation about something that might upset him, given he'd kept it a secret from her for years.

But today was a new day, and he looked pretty chipper. Her discovery about him going to medical school was burning a hole in her brain. They needed to talk. Right now.

"Hey, Dad." She moved closer to the bed. "How're you feeling?"

"Aside from them keeping me in this damn bed, I'm fine."

Good. Complaints. That meant he was feeling better. "Now, now," she soothed, straightening the blanket at the end of his bed. "They just want to be sure you're okay before they let you move around much."

"Or feed me decent food," he groused. "You wouldn't believe what passes for a meal around here."

"Yes, well, you'd better get used to a different lifestyle. Dr. Phelps has made it clear your diet has to change and you have to lose some weight to stay healthy."

He crossed his arms over his broad chest. "I know, I know. Low fat, low cholesterol and all that." He made a face. "Sounds awful."

Jill sat in the chair next to the bed, resisting the urge to lecture him about his diet right now. There would be plenty of time to get the point across after he was released from the hospital.

Besides, she had more pressing matters to talk about. "Listen, Dad, when I talked to Dr. Phelps he told me that you and he went to medical school together."

Her dad's eyes went wide and he stilled. After a moment he nodded. "Yes, we did."

"Why didn't you ever tell me that?"

He shrugged. "Didn't seem relevant. It was a long time ago, in another life, really."

"Why didn't you become a doctor?"

He shifted in his bed. "Well, I was going to, and your mother and I, with you, of course, were getting ready to move to L.A. from Seattle for my residency." His eyes reflected a resigned sadness. "But then your mom was killed and I knew there was no way I could handle the demands of a residency and a baby. So I moved back here where I'd grown up, and instead of being a doctor, I pursued my other passion, something I'd been interested in since I was a boy."

"Inventing," Jill said in a monotone, her stomach twisting. The thing that had made her the butt of so many jokes.

He nodded. "Yes, inventing. I'd always loved it, and it was an occupation that allowed me to be at home with you." He smiled, his face glowing. "I've been happy with my choice, and quite successful, too, if I do say so myself. I've never had to take another job to support us."

Jill sagged back in her chair, self-recriminations marching through her. "You sacrificed your career as a physician for me," she whispered, meeting his gaze. "I never knew that."

He reached out a hand for her.

She took it, holding on tight.

"I've never regretted my decision, Jilly-girl, never saw it as a sacrifice. Just what I needed to do to make sure you had the best life possible."

Shame reverberated inside her like an explosion. She'd been selfish. Judgmental. Critical. A terrible daughter.

Now it was time for some good old-fashioned honesty. It was the least her dad deserved. "Do you know I've always been bothered by the fact that you

were an inventor rather than something more traditional like a banker or lawyer?"

"Sure, sure, I knew that." He patted her hand.
"Kids can be cruel, and my nickname sure didn't
help, did it?"

She shook her head, smiling ruefully. "No, it didn't."

"I regret you had to put up with that kind of
teasing, and for that, I'm sorry. But, you know, the
joking around never bothered me on a personal level.
I know who I am and what I'm capable of, and I *am*
a wacky kind of guy. The nickname makes sense, and
I embraced it a long time ago."

His words soaking in, Jill looked around the
room, again noting all the flowers, balloons and get-
well cards from people, she realized, who cared
about him. Obviously many people in town considered him a friend. A sharp-edged, painful thought
slammed into her, taking her breath away.

The truth was, *she* was really the only one around
who didn't have any respect for what he did.

Mortification and cutting shame ate at her all over
again, more cruel than ever before.

She pressed a shaking hand to her lips. She hated
to find that she'd been such a selfish idiot about her
dad. But she'd discovered the truth, and she deserved
the searing guilt knifing through her.

She embraced that pain as her due, swearing that
she would learn from it and grow as a person.

In that vein, when she thought about it, her need
for the town's respect seemed pretty darned insignif-

icant compared not only to almost losing her dad, but also to the sacrifice he'd made.

All in the name of his love for her.

Something shifted inside her, and the resentment she'd always felt toward her dad faded away and lost all of its sharp edges. The love that had been overshadowed by it shone through like the sun breaking from behind the clouds on a cold winter day.

Succeeding in business for the sole purpose of gaining the town's respect didn't seem so all-consuming any longer. Sure, she wanted to do well at her chosen job. It was her livelihood, and she took great pride in what she could accomplish, and always would. But she saw now that it was more important to respect herself—as her dad respected himself—than it was to prove herself to anyone else.

She squeezed her dad's meaty hand. "I'm sorry that I didn't respect your job."

He waved his free hand in the air. "I know I'm a bit eccentric, and not everybody understands that." He smiled, waggling his eyebrows. "Occupational hazard."

Her heart lightened. "You've opened my eyes today, Dad." She stood and pressed a kiss to his stubbly cheek, then pulled back and looked into his blue eyes. "Thank you."

He pressed a hand to the side of her head. "Can I open your eyes about something else?"

She nodded. "Sure."

"Don't let a good man like Brandon Clark get away."

She blinked. "What?"

"You heard me, Jilly." He pointed a rigid finger at her. "I know that scumbag Doug did a number on you and I know you've been avoiding letting yourself get close to a man because you don't want to get hurt again. But Brandon is a good man, and I think he cares about you. I think he's worth the risk."

Her heart pounded. "Why do you think he cares about me?"

"I saw the way he looked at you the day you guys found the girls at my apartment." His eyes grew misty. "It was the same way I looked at your mother, and I loved her with all my heart."

Jill sank into the chair, feeling suddenly warm and light-headed. So her dad thought Brandon loved her. But her dad was an idealist from way back, and often read into people's emotions things that weren't there. While she wanted to believe him with every-thing in her, he wasn't a particularly reliable source.

Even so, was it possible Brandon cared about her?

She shook her head. No, no, she couldn't let herself believe that.

Because she wasn't sure she had the guts to risk loving him back.

Brandon raised his fist and knocked gently on the door of hospital room 405.

He hoped Jill was here. He'd just heard about Mr.

Winters's heart attack this morning from Kristy and he regretted he hadn't shown up here sooner to offer Jill support.

He only hoped he could keep his thoughts strictly platonic when, like an idiot, all he'd been able to think about lately was convincing her to knock down the wall she'd erected around her heart and let him in. Feelings were feelings. He loved her.

"Come in," Jill called.

He pushed the door open and stepped into Mr. Winters's hospital room. Jill sat in an ugly brown chair next to the empty bed, dark circles immediately noticeable beneath her blue eyes, her cheeks pale, her hair scraped back into a messy ponytail. She stood when she saw him, her hands clenched in a knot at her slender waist.

Empty bed...

Oh, no. His chest collapsing, he rushed to her and immediately took her in his arms. "Did he...?"

She pulled back, a quizzical look on her face. Then she smiled. "No, no, he's fine."

Relief gushed through him. He looked at the empty bed. "Where is he?"

"Having some tests."

"Are you okay?" he asked, again noting how haggard and tired she looked. How could he have forgotten how good she felt in his arms, so small and warm and perfect?

She nodded against his chest. "Now that I know he's going to be all right, I am."

"So he's going to recover?"

"Yes, he should be fine if he changes his diet, exercises and loses some weight." She looked up and rolled her eyes. "He's been grousing about that nonstop."

"Why didn't you call me when you found out?" he asked, reaching up to stroke her velvet-smooth cheek. "I'm sorry that I wasn't here yesterday."

She closed her eyes briefly, as if she was gathering her strength. Then she took a deep breath and stepped back and away, her mouth rigid. "I didn't want to bother you."

"Like being here for you is a bother?" he asked, jerking his hands to his hips. "Is that what you really think? At the very least I could have helped out with Zoe."

She looked at the floor, then wandered over and gazed out the window, turning her back to him. "Mel—from the restaurant—helped out with Zoe," she said. "Besides, I wasn't…comfortable asking for your help."

An ache grew in his chest. She was putting space between her heart and his. He should be glad; he needed to be more cautious, more protective of himself where she was concerned. But her shutting him out hurt, dammit. Maybe he was a glutton for punishment. Maybe he just wasn't ready to give up on her yet.

"You are so stubborn. Why do you keep building so many walls between us?" he blurted, then wished he could call the words back. Trying to reason with her was a waste of time. And he certainly hadn't come here to have a major confrontation just when she needed some calm in her life.

He also was sure that her stubborn refusal to let him into her heart would nail him in the end. Too bad his judgment where Jill was concerned was shot clear to hell. She had a way of making him forget about being smart.

She raised her chin. "I have no idea what you're talking about."

He clenched his jaw, then moved over to stand in back of her, barely managing not to touch her. "Oh, come on, Jill. I know why you can't let yourself become romantically involved with me, but I don't see why we can't at least be friends." He was willing to give it a shot if it meant keeping her in his life one way or another.

She didn't respond right away. Then she turned around and looked at him, shaking her head. "I can't be friends with a man I've kissed," she said, pushing her nose in the air, a light blush staining her cheeks. "Besides, are you sure being just friends would be enough for you?"

He remembered their kiss, and warmth bloomed down low. He ignored that hot ache and her question and asked his own instead, giving in to his deepest fantasy. "Are you saying that being friends wouldn't be enough for *you?*"

"What I might want in some foolish piece of my

heart and what I can actually have are two different things."

His fragile, irrational hopes took flight, lighting up a tiny corner of his heart, goading him to go on when he should probably just back off and be content with simply being her occasional friend. "So you're admitting that somewhere inside you you want to be more than friends?"

She shook her head, the corners of her lips downturned. "I'll say it again. What I might want in my wildest dreams and what I can actually have aren't the same thing, Brandon. I wish they were, but they're not."

Her words zinged right into his heart, slicing deep, snuffing out that dim light of hope. He rubbed the bridge of his nose. "So you're still too afraid to take a chance on me, aren't you?" he asked, his frustration over her bullheadedness making his words harsher than he'd intended. "Still afraid to put your heart on the line?"

She glowered at him, then started pacing. "I'm not afraid—"

He cut her off by grabbing her hands and making her hold still. "Yes, you are, Jill. And I get that. But can't you see that I would never, ever hurt you?" He held back telling her he loved her, afraid she'd bolt from the room and he'd never see her again, which would be worse than being relegated to the status of friend.

Wouldn't it?

She stared at him, her mouth a tight line. "Words

aren't enough, Brandon. I didn't think Doug would ever hurt me, but he did, and now I can't take the risk. I have to protect myself. I don't know any other way."

The pain he was expecting hit him dead-on, giving a one-two punch to his heart all over again. But he fought the hurt back, trying to take away its control and ability to bring him to his knees. Call him a dreamer, but he was unable to totally give up on Jill.

"Do you have any idea what you're walking away from?" he asked, squeezing her hands, his voice low and intense. "Any idea how much you're giving up?"

Tears bloomed in her eyes. "Of course I know," she said, her voice cracking. "But knowing doesn't change anything. I fear what I fear, end of story. I'm sorry."

The ache he'd fought back consumed him, working its way through his soul like a black tide, mixing with regret for upsetting her and making her cry. Why had he gone down this road when it was so difficult, so damn futile, for them both? How big a fool was he?

Fool, yes, and a man who had to be sure his love for her was futile before he walked away. But he was also smart enough to know when to gather up his toys and go home.

He let the searing pain caused by her rejection burrow into his heart so there would be no expectations for a happily-ever-after left in his mind. He had to get the message that Jill wasn't ever going to love him, no matter how much he loved her. She'd made her choice. He had to accept it.

Forcing himself to cut his losses while he was still standing, he very deliberately let go of her small, soft hands, severing their connection. If nothing else, he would walk away for Jill's sake. This was what she wanted, though the knowledge did little to soothe the agonizing ache in his heart.

Jill's heart turned ice-cold. A deep, abiding sense of hopelessness and loss moved through her. Oh, how she wanted to fling herself into Brandon's arms and take whatever he offered.

But the hole Doug had cut in her heart wouldn't let her.

And Brandon. She wanted to trust him. Badly. But she couldn't ignore the fact that he could up and move again, or could be using her to gain an advantage with The Steak Place.

As much as she hated it, she just couldn't hand him on a silver platter the power to hurt or betray her.

Or could she? Was she really prepared to walk away from him? Forever?

Those questions roiled around inside her like a dark, conflicted brew.

She was so, so afraid—both to love him and to lose him. And that was a weird, confusing combination that froze her in limbo, afraid to go forward or back away.

She drank in the sight of him, admiring his dark

eyes and wavy dark brown hair. His genuine concern for her touched her deep within.

Her heart melted. He was a good man, probably the best man she'd ever met, and a great father, too. He was loving, considerate, kind and generous.

She'd dreamed of him being here with her, had wished he would show up and take her in his arms and help her through this crisis. Now he was standing in front of her, of his own accord. She had to say something….

But what? Confessing all her doubts and fears was such a risk, such a dangerous place for her to go. He hadn't given her anything concrete to hang her hopes on.

Her nagging fears took over again and her throat closed over, silencing her. She struggled against those paralyzing fears, still so unsure of which way to go.

But she had to make a choice. Right now, before Brandon took away from her that chance to choose.

Before she could force words out, his eyes frosted over and he intoned, "Well, I guess that's it." He stepped back, then turned and headed to the door, his shoulders stiff. "I'd better get going."

Stomach-munching panic filled her, cutting off her breath, making her feel sick. She needed more time. "Brandon, wait…"

He turned with his hand on the door, his face totally devoid of emotion. "Yes?" he asked in a monotone.

This was her chance. Her last-ditch moment to

embrace whatever nebulous feelings she had for him and tell him the truth.

The truth.

Trouble was, she didn't know the truth, hadn't had time to tame her nagging fears and figure it out without the stress of her dad's condition influencing her.

She opened her mouth to ask him to stay and be her shoulder to lean on. But the words froze on her tongue. It was all happening too fast and Brandon was coming at her when she was already feeling so vulnerable about her dad, when her world was still turned upside down.

Was this really a good time to make such a world-altering decision, a decision that would have deep ramifications not only for her, but for Zoe, Kristy and Brandon, too?

No, she had to wait until she was on more firm emotional ground to consider letting Brandon have free rein over her heart, and vice versa. She owed them both that.

"Thank you for coming," she forced herself to say. "I...appreciate your concern."

A muscle in his jaw ticked, then he nodded, one short, curt bob of his head. "No problem. Let me know if you need help with Zoe."

And then he was gone.

Leaving Jill all alone.

Funny. That was how she'd thought she needed to be. Alone. Safe.

Then why did she hurt so much? Why did she feel

as if he'd yanked out her heart and taken it with him? As if she'd never be happy again?

She sat down and dropped her head into her hands, her eyes burning.

Had she just made one giant, painful mistake?

Chapter Ten

Brandon looked up from the blueprints he was going over at the restaurant with the general contractor and saw Gene Hobart, his landlord, walking toward him. Gene wore his trademark olive-green fedora over his too long gray hair and a green houndstooth, elbow-patched blazer with a satin, cream-colored handkerchief in the breast pocket. Brandon noted he'd grown a goatee in the weeks since he'd leased his restaurant space from him.

Brandon held back a snicker and rolled his eyes. Hobart clearly thought he was the big-shot business mogul of Elm Corners when, in truth, he was really just a small-potatoes property owner with grand delusions and even bigger pretensions.

"Gene," Brandon said, moving out from behind

the counter he'd spread the blueprints on. "What can I do for you?"

Gene cast his snooty gaze around. "The place is really shaping up well."

Brandon propped his hands on his hips. "Thanks. I should be ready to open in a few weeks."

"I'll be one of your first customers." Gene put one hand in his blazer pocket. "Listen, I'm coming to you with an offer."

"Shoot," Brandon said, his curiosity rising.

"Jill Lindstrom's lease is up soon, and before I renegotiate it with her, I thought I'd give you first crack."

A sick feeling moved through Brandon. Though he hadn't seen Jill since he'd gone to see her at her dad's hospital room two days ago, she'd been on his mind. A lot. Probably too much, considering his love for her was so damn one-sided.

He dragged his thoughts away from how his heart still ached from losing Jill and focused on Gene instead. "Why don't you want to renew her lease?"

"It's not exactly that I don't want to," Gene assured him. "More that I—"

"Can make more money off me," Brandon shot back, raising his brows to a sharp angle.

Hobart lifted a slim shoulder, his dark eyes blasé. "I'm a businessman, not a charitable institution, Brandon, and I know you can afford more than Jill can. So yes, I can charge you more. Wanting that kind of deal is just good business, that's all."

Brandon held in an oath. He doubted Jill would see it that way. Gene coming to him with this deal would ruin her. Brandon wanted to shove Hobart's *good business* right up his nose.

But he didn't. Gene was, unfortunately, the man he had to deal with to make his dreams of opening a restaurant come true, so he resisted the urge to do Hobart bodily harm on Jill's behalf. He had to think about what the man was offering him.

More space for The Steak Place, which was what Brandon had wanted to begin with, not to mention the chance to edge Jill out of the restaurant business before he'd even opened. With The Wildflower Grill gone from the fine-dining picture in Elm Corners, his business would undoubtedly go gangbusters right out of the gate.

He'd be an almost guaranteed success. His dreams of being a successful restaurateur would come true and he'd be able to stay in Elm Corners, where Kristy was thriving.

Well, at least some of the things he was hoping for would come true. But one fantasy sure wouldn't be a reality—the dream of him and Jill having any kind of future.

Curse her streak of stubbornness. He pictured Jill holding up that damn album, declaring that she could never love again. Then he recalled how she'd told him in her dad's hospital room that what she wanted and what she could have weren't the same thing. Talk about a killer comment.

Then he remembered how his heart had crumbled each time she'd told him to take a hike. How despite her rejections he'd dreamed of her every night since. How he longed to see her, hold her, be with her forever.

He snorted under his breath. All of those yearnings and hopes were futile and impossible. Jill wasn't able—or willing—to get around her past long enough to love him.

Bitterness worked its way through him, clawing at his insides, telling him this was his chance to get back at Jill.

To hurt her the way she'd hurt him.

Yeah, damn her, he hurt. A deep, agonizing pain that cut him like a white-hot knife blade. Almost as much as his futile love for her glowed bright and true.

He turned to Hobart and did the only thing he could possibly do. "We need to talk, Gene. Right now."

Jill sat down in the chair across from Gene Hobart, pen in hand. "I'm ready to sign."

"How's your dad doing?" he asked as he set the lease agreement on the desk in front of her.

Appreciating Gene's concern, she looked at him rather than going over the paperwork just yet. "He came home this morning, and aside from some very loud complaining about all of the heart-healthy foods now in his cupboard and refrigerator, he's fine."

Gene nodded, but there was something in his expression that made him seem less than sincere. "Glad to hear it."

Jill read the lease over to be sure it contained the appropriate details. When she was assured it did, she signed it, happy to have her restaurant space locked up and leased for the next two years.

She only hoped she'd be in business another two years. With Brandon only weeks away from opening, who knew how she'd be doing in six months?

Either psychologically or in the business arena.

She'd been an emotional wreck since she'd gone mute from confused, conflicted feelings and let him walk out of her dad's hospital room two days ago. She simply hadn't been able to shake the feeling that she'd made a huge blunder by holding back with Brandon.

But she'd been so afraid to really examine her feelings for him that she hadn't done anything about talking to him. No, sir. She'd taken the chicken's way out and had focused all her energy on her dad's recovery instead of figuring out what to do about Brandon.

If she was going to do anything at all. She'd protected herself for so long she was scared spitless to take a flying leap, spill her guts and tell him he was the most wonderful man she'd ever met and to never leave her side.

She handed Gene the lease. "There you go. Another two years taken care of."

He took the paperwork from her. "Yes, indeed. Lucky for you Brandon Clark isn't a very cutthroat competitor. Bad for me, though. I could have made a lot more on him."

She frowned. "Excuse me? What does Brandon have to do with this lease?"

"Oh, just that he refused my offer to take over the lease of your space this morning."

"What?" she barked, snapping to attention.

"I offered him this space and he turned it down. Said he cared for and respected you too much to take the deal." He smirked. "Now, that's what I call a friend…or whatever."

Jill let her jaw sag. Brandon had turned down the opportunity to lease her space?

"I can see you're surprised," Gene said, leaning forward. "Must be some pretty personal feelings simmering between you and Clark. Are you two more than just business competitors?"

Jill snapped her jaw closed. Not only was Gene a self-proclaimed natty dresser and a pretentious airbag, he was also well-known as an avid local rumormonger. She suspected he'd told her about Brandon to gain some prurient details about their relationship, and maybe also to make her regret she couldn't afford to pay more for her space.

Why, the scheming, low-down gossip. She'd be a fool to let Gene in on anything personal.

Attempting to downplay how stunned she was that Brandon had turned down the lease—for her sake, apparently—she rearranged her face into a neutral expression.

After a few seconds she took a deep breath and shot Gene a hard glare. "So let me get this straight,

Gene," she said, rising so she could be in the position of power. "You offered him my space?"

He held up his hands, looking not the least bit sorry. "Hey, Jill, I'm a savvy businessman, and Brandon has deeper pockets than you do. No shame in pursuing that, especially since there was nothing in your contract preventing me from doing so."

"I think that depends on your perspective," she said dryly, turning to go. She had more important things to think about than Gene's sleazy business ethics. "Remind me *not* to send you a Christmas gift this year."

Gene sputtered, but she ignored him and left his office, her legs wobbly.

She stepped out onto the rustic boardwalk that lined Elm Corners' main drag, then sank onto a wooden bench sitting against the wall between Gene's office and Emma Lou's Bakery.

A hot chill ran through her and her heart throbbed. Brandon had given up leasing her space. For her.

Incredible. Unbelievable. Fantastic.

She pressed a shaking hand to her lips. She couldn't ignore that he was a man full of integrity and honor who had put her needs first. She knew how much he wanted to succeed in Elm Corners, and why. For Kristy. For himself. He'd sacrificed the chance to be the only fine-dining player in town at the possible expense of his own wants and needs.

And he'd done it for *her.*

Her chest constricted. Was she willing to give up

such a wonderful, considerate, absolutely perfect guy, one who had been thinking of her above his own success, simply because Doug had dumped her? She let out a heavy breath. Wouldn't that be giving Doug much more power over her than she should?

What had seemed so clear a week ago—keep Brandon out of her heart at all costs—suddenly wasn't so clear anymore. She'd built a hundred walls to keep him at a distance, but those walls had tumbled down today and didn't mean diddly-squat anymore.

What mattered was…well, she'd learned a lot of things in the past few days. First, she'd learned from her dear old dad, and Brandon, too, that her path in life might not always be what she expected or planned—and that that was okay. Look at how well both of them had done when life had thrown them the worst of unexpected curves. They'd both picked up the pieces after their wives had died, changed course and found a way to thrive. They were both profound testimony to adapting and adjusting and moving on when the chips were down or life became a challenge.

She wanted to take that concept to heart. And she finally felt strong and whole enough to do it.

Second, she'd learned despite her hard head and stubborn, frightened heart that Brandon was a one-in-a-million guy she'd be a fool to give up.

Oh, my. More hot chills ran up her spine.

She loved him. Desperately.

And she had grown and changed enough to finally be willing to fully own the emotion instead of skating around it as she'd been doing for days.

Her heart thrummed again and she felt light-headed. Her brain was stuffed full and reeling from all the discoveries she'd made today.

But one thought rang clear. The thought of living without Brandon was much scarier than the thought of taking the risk to have him in her life—forever.

She stood, gaining strength from the depth of her feelings. A shiver of fear ripped through her, but she ignored it. She had to put her heart on the line even though Brandon had only hinted at his feelings. He could very well throw her love right back in her face, given how many times she'd cut him off at the knees.

It was a risk she had to take.

For herself. For Brandon.

For the rare, precious love she'd never expected to find.

Brandon climbed out of his SUV in front of Jill's two-story, light blue Victorian-style house, the light drizzle and gray clouds perfectly matching his frame of mind.

He slammed the SUV's door and trudged up the cement walkway to the front door, his mood black. He not only had Jill occupying most of his mind. Clutched in his fist he also had the physical proof of Kristy's and Zoe's stubborn refusal to forget their stupid plan to invent a family.

Clenching his jaw, he remembered what the note said:

> Go to the Lindstroms' house to invent a
> family.

The note, which was printed on a plain white sheet of paper as all of the girls' other notes had been, had no signature. But, damn, he knew who had written it, and why. Despite the punishment he'd doled out to Kristy—a week's grounding and extra chores around the house—she and Zoe were still hell-bent on getting him and Jill together.

He let out a derisive snort. Their plan was futile. While he loved Jill with his whole heart and soul, she didn't love him. Or wouldn't. Or couldn't. Whatever. The bald, painful truth was that they were never going to be a couple.

Since they'd talked in the hospital, he'd thought about cornering her and begging her to reconsider. But he hadn't, because he didn't want to put Jill in that kind of awkward position. He loved her enough to give her the space she needed. Even if that meant going through the rest of his life alone.

A bleak picture, yes. But he was a realist. She'd made her choice, and even though it ripped his insides to shreds to think about living without her, he had to accept the truth and deal with it. How he was going to do that when he ached for her every minute of the day he had no idea.

He reached the porch and stopped at the white wooden door. Subduing the burning regret in his heart, he raised a fist and knocked on the door harder than he probably should have. The sooner he picked up Kristy, left and gave her a piece of his mind, the better.

A few seconds later Jill answered the door. She looked wonderful in a pair of dark jeans and an ocean-blue sweater that matched her eyes perfectly. She'd left her hair down to fall in soft golden waves about her slim shoulders.

His chest ached. How was he going to pick up Kristy and see Jill without taking a knife in the heart every time? Even so, he wouldn't deny his daughter her friendship with Zoe or the presence of Jill in her life in at least a small measure.

Jill gave him a shy smile, but actually looked happy to see him. "Brandon. Hi."

His heart shriveled a bit more. She put on a pretty good show for a woman who had blatantly refused to open her heart up to him.

"Hey, Jill," he managed. He held up the crumpled letter. "They're at it again. I found this letter in my kitchen when I got home from work."

Strangely, she smiled and her eyes brightened. "Why don't you come in and we'll…talk about it." She stepped back and gestured for him to come in.

He walked by her into the house, swiping a hand across his face. "I punished Kristy—severely. I can't imagine why she and Zoe would keep at this when we've told them so many times to stop." He looked around the entryway. "Where is she? I'll just get her, go home and lock her up for a few years."

Jill reached out and touched his arm. "The girls are in Zoe's room." She paced away, then turned around and took in a huge breath. "They didn't send you the note."

He pulled back his chin. "Then who did?"

She took his hand.

His heart squeezed at her touch. What was going on?

Her cheeks pinkened. "Uh...I did."

He stared at her, certain he'd misheard. "You did? Why would you do that?"

She grabbed his other hand—he could feel her shaking—then stepped in close, so close he could smell her flowery perfume and see the dark flecks of blue in her eyes. "Because I want to invent a family. With you."

The proverbial truck walloped him from behind. His heart slammed into his ribs. He couldn't swallow. "You're joking, right?" he choked out. That was the only explanation, the only possible truth he would let himself believe.

She let go of his hands, only to smooth her own up his chest to his shoulders, setting fires along the way. Then she looked deep into his eyes and said, "I love you, Brandon, and I don't ever want to be without you. Can you forgive me for being so stubborn and idiotic and scared?"

He wanted to believe her, with everything in him. He stared at her, looking for the truth. He saw the firm set of her jaw and how she looked right at him, saw the serene smile on her face.

And saw the love burning in her eyes.

Love for...*him.*

Pure joy crashed through him, chasing away the ache he'd lived with for days. Weeks. Years.

"Aren't you going to say anything?" she asked in a small voice.

He slid his arms around her slender back and pulled her close so he could whisper in her ear. "I'm speechless."

She pulled away and looked up at him, worry now reflected in her eyes. "I'm afraid that you won't want me since I...was such an idiot all those times you tried to convince me to give you a chance."

"Well, I'm not *that* speechless," he said, smoothing a hand through her soft, silky hair. "I want you more than I've ever wanted anything, and I'm just glad you finally decided to give me—us—a chance."

Her shoulders relaxed and her eyes softened. On tiptoes she leaned close. "Oh, good," she murmured in his ear. "Then why don't we do this?" And then she kissed her way across his cheek to his mouth.

He groaned and met her kiss, unbelievable happiness filling him to overflowing. As always, she felt perfect in his arms, as if she were made solely for him.

After a long, deep kiss, he nuzzled her sweet-smelling neck. "What made you change your mind?"

"You did."

He looked down into her sparkling eyes. "How?"

"By refusing to take Gene up on his offer."

"How do you know about that?" he asked.

"Gene told me."

"That sleazeball." He ground out the words. "What kind of guy boasts about his crummy business ethics?"

She shook her head and pressed a warm hand to Brandon's tight jaw. "No, it's all right. I'm glad he told me. If he hadn't I might never have come to my senses and realized that I'd be a fool to walk away from a man who would sacrifice his own success for me."

"I want you to be happy, Jill," he said, caressing her cheek. "I love you, more than I ever believed possible."

She grinned. "Well then, it's fortunate you're here, Mr. Clark, because you make me happier than anyone in the whole world."

He kissed her again, over and over, his heart beating in time with hers. When he was breathless and warm and drowning in her he pressed a few hot kisses to her face. "How about we become one big, happy family?"

"Oh, Brandon," she breathed, tears forming in her eyes. "That sounds absolutely perfect."

"I was hoping you'd see it that way." He gave her a huge smile. "And how about we knock down some walls and open one huge restaurant that we can run together?"

Her face lit up. "Excellent idea. I'll be the brains and you'll be the—"

Loud giggles interrupted Jill. He turned to see Kristy and Zoe peeking out through the stairway banister.

"You guys are kissing," Zoe said, beaming from ear to ear. "Does that mean you love each other?"

Brandon pulled Jill close. "It sure does," he said, genuine happiness and contentment flooding his entire soul.

Zoe and Kristy cheered, then raced down the stairs and flung themselves at him and Jill, jumping up and down, babbling about finally being real sisters.

Brandon pulled all of his girls close, his heart bursting, finally whole. He'd found a woman he loved who, miraculously, loved him back. Before long, Kristy would have a new sister and a mom.

He was a lucky, lucky man.

Thank goodness their daughters hadn't listened to them and quit scheming. If they had, he might never have fallen in love with Jill.

He met her ecstatic blue gaze and returned her bright, happy smile.

He couldn't think of a better invention than a family that included them all.

* * * * *

SILHOUETTE *Romance*®

A family saga begins to unravel
when the doors to the Bella Lucia
Restaurant Empire are opened...

The Brides of Bella Lucia

A family torn apart by secrets,
reunited by marriage

AUGUST 2006

COMING HOME TO THE COWBOY
by Patricia Thayer

Find out what happens to Rebecca Valentine when
her relationship with a millionaire cowboy and single
dad moves from professional to personal.

SEPTEMBER 2006

The Valentine family saga continues in

HARLEQUIN® *Romance*

with **THE REBEL PRINCE** by Raye Morgan

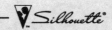

SPECIAL EDITION™

Welcome to Danbury Way—where nothing is as it seems...

Megan Schumacher has managed to maintain a low profile on Danbury Way by keeping the huge success of her graphics business a secret. But when a new client turns out to be a neighbor's sexy ex-husband, rumors of their developing romance quickly start to swirl.

THE RELUCTANT CINDERELLA

by CHRISTINE RIMMER

Available July 2006

Don't miss the first book from the Talk of the Neighborhood miniseries.

The Marian priestesses were destroyed long ago,
but their daughters live on. The time has come
for the heiresses to learn of their legacy, to unite
the pieces of a powerful mosaic and bring light to
a secret their ancestors died to protect.

The Madonna Key

Follow their quests each month.

Page-turning drama…

Exotic, glamorous locations…

Intense emotion and passionate seduction…

Sheikhs, princes and billionaire tycoons…

This summer, may we suggest:

THE SHEIKH'S DISOBEDIENT BRIDE
by Jane Porter
On sale June.

AT THE GREEK TYCOON'S BIDDING
by Cathy Williams
On sale July.

THE ITALIAN MILLIONAIRE'S VIRGIN WIFE
On sale August.

With new titles to choose from every month, discover a world of romance in our books written by internationally bestselling authors.

HARLEQUIN *Presents*

It's the ultimate in quality romance!

Available wherever Harlequin books are sold.

www.eHarlequin.com

HPGEN06

HOTEL MARCHAND

Four sisters.
A family legacy.
And someone is out to destroy it.

A captivating new limited continuity, launching June 2006

The most beautiful hotel in New Orleans,
and someone is out to destroy it. But mystery,
danger and some surprising family revelations
and discoveries won't stop the Marchand sisters
from protecting their birthright…
and finding love along the way.

SPECIAL PRICE!

This riveting new saga begins with

by national bestselling author

JUDITH ARNOLD

The party at Hotel Marchand
is in full swing when the lights
suddenly go out. What does
head of security Mac Jensen
do first? He's torn between two
jobs — protecting the guests
at the hotel and keeping the
woman he loves safe.

A woman to protect. A hotel
to secure. And no idea who's
determined to harm them.

On Sale June 2006

COMING NEXT MONTH

#1822 PRICELESS GIFTS—Cara Colter
A Father's Wish

Sure her father is trying to keep her safe from some crazed stalker, but firing her staff and removing her from her luxury suite to her crazy aunt's farm is going too far! Chelsea King is pretty sure the situation can't get any worse—until she meets her new bodyguard, Randall Peabody. An ex-soldier—broken, scarred, protective— Randall stirs something in Chelsea and makes her feel as if she hasn't really lived until now....

#1823 THE BRIDE'S BEST MAN—Judy Christenberry

Logic and order are Shelby Cook's typical, lawyerly methods. But when she goes with her aunt on a much-needed vacation to Hawaii, she never expects to meet her long-lost father and to be attracted to his friend Pete Campbell. Shelby doesn't think the attraction will go anywhere, but Pete is about to show her that true love defies all limitations and logic!

#1824 ONE MAN AND A BABY—Susan Meier
The Cupid Campaign

Experience has taught Ashley Meljac not to trust her instincts regarding men, especially when it comes to the town's resident bad boy—Rick Capriotti. Still, something in the way he cares for his baby makes her forget the past and dream about a future with him and his adorable toddler....

#1825 HERE WITH ME—Holly Jacobs

After divorce and a miscarriage, Lee Singer just craves quiet and solitude. But soon Adam Benton, a workaholic with a one-year-old in tow, arrives back in town. And all too soon he's brought noise and life to her world and got her questioning what she truly desires.